Keepers

A Love Story

Rebecca G. Hooper

OUTER RIDGE PRESS

Keepers

A Love Story

Rebecca G. Hooper

ISBN: 979-8-9986024-0-5 (Paperback)

ISBN: (eBook)

This is Book One of the Keepers Trilogy.

Copyright © 2025 Rebecca G. Hooper

All Rights Reserved.

Edited by: Ita de Groot

Printed in the United States of America

OUTER RIDGE PRESS
www.outerridgepress.com

Table of Contents

Chapter 1

Raleigh in April

"That's enough for reports," Emma sighed, hitting 'Enter' on her keyboard. The mechanical click of the keys and the soft hum of the computer filled the quiet office. Her stomach grumbled, a low, insistent growl that reminded her it was time for lunch. Glancing at the clock, she saw it was nearly noon, the digital numbers glowing green against the dim office lighting.

She turned to the officer in the next cubicle. "I'm running out for lunch. Meeting Dave," she said, peeking over the gray partition at Steve, a fellow patrol officer. The artificial light overhead cast a faint glare on his computer screen, reflecting the spreadsheets he was reviewing.

"Take care," Steve mumbled without looking up, his fingers clacking away at the keyboard. The faint scent of stale coffee and printer ink lingered in the air.

1

Emma grabbed her jacket and walked out the side door of the police station. The moment she stepped outside, the warmth of the midday sun wrapped around her, a welcome contrast to the cool, controlled climate inside. The scent of freshly cut grass mixed with the light floral fragrance of blooming azaleas. As she passed a row of vibrant pink blossoms and pear trees, the soft rustling of leaves whispered in the gentle breeze. She couldn't help but smile.

"I love Raleigh in April," she murmured to herself, breathing in the crisp, sweet air. "The azaleas are perfect this time of year."

She climbed into her patrol car, the fabric seat slightly warm from the sun, and started the engine. The low rumble of the vehicle vibrated through her hands as she gripped the steering wheel. The familiar scent of leather and the faint hint of fast-food fries from an old takeout bag filled the car. She adjusted her rearview mirror before pulling out onto the road, the rhythmic clicking of the turn signal punctuating the moment.

Earlier that morning, Dave, her partner for over two years, had called to remind her of his dentist appointment. He'd meet her later for lunch.

Dave and Emma had gone through the police academy together—Emma joining straight out of college and Dave returning from a tour in Iraq with the United States Army at Fort Bragg, North Carolina. Though five years older, Dave respected Emma's sharp instincts and unrelenting determination. Over time, they'd developed a partnership built on mutual trust.

Emma's connection to the police force ran deep. At 24, with striking auburn hair that gleamed like burnished copper in the sunlight and clear blue eyes, she had risen to the top of her academy class. Her father, Ryan Patterson, had been a respected

2

officer on the Raleigh Police Force for twenty-five years. From a young age, Emma had been by his side—whether fishing, hiking, or talking shop. She admired him deeply and had always dreamed of following in his footsteps.

Ryan Patterson was a name known far and wide, a true legend on the force. In 2008, he negotiated a tense hostage situation at the Raleigh Bank of America, where a desperate man had taken thirty-three hostages. The bank had been eerily silent, save for the nervous shuffling of hostages and the occasional sharp command from the gunman. The air inside had been thick with fear, the metallic scent of perspiration hanging heavily in the confined space.

Ryan recognized the fear in the robber's eyes—a man who needed to be heard, not harmed, someone in need of help, not a bullet. Of Scottish descent, Ryan had a gift for storytelling that could capture a listener's ear and weave a cocoon of calm around them.

He shared a tale, a metaphor about a crow on a hot summer's day, dying of thirst. The bird was moments away from death, yearning for water from a bottle—but the water was low, and the bottle's opening too narrow. Ryan spun the story of how the crow found small pebbles and dropped them into the bottle, one by one, causing the water to rise slowly. Inch by inch, the water level crept higher, and the crow, desperate for a drink, could see the end of its struggle in sight.

As Ryan spoke, the tension in the bank began to fade. The story not only soothed the robber but also calmed the hostages, each one drawn into the metaphor. With the final pebble dropped, the water reached the top of the bottle, and the crow drank, its thirst finally quenched—its life spared. Ryan explained that while the crow was certainly in dire straits, it used its wits to find another way to survive. "There's always a good option," Ryan said, his voice steady. "One that's best. Don't you agree? Let's take the best option today so we can all walk out of here… and not be carried out."

The robber hesitated, then lowered his weapon, pushing it toward Ryan. A wave of relief washed over the hostages. Ryan signaled for them to leave the bank while he stayed behind with the young man. By the end of the standoff, the robber had surrendered peacefully, walking out without a shot being fired. Ryan's de-escalation skills had saved lives. It was a triumph, but one that would mark the beginning of the strain that would weigh on him in the years to come.

Ryan had a long and storied career with the Raleigh Police Department, though not every encounter with criminals ended as peacefully as he would have liked. Late in his career, he was shot in the upper left arm while on duty. The bullet had burned like fire, the sharp pain radiating down to his fingertips. The scent of gunpowder had clung to his uniform long after the incident. It was a wound that kept him in the hospital for a brief time, but he made a full recovery and returned to work, undeterred by the danger he had faced.

When retirement came, Ryan and his wife Erin left the bustling city of Raleigh for a quieter life in Linville, North Carolina. They moved to the farm where Erin had grown up, nestled along the peaceful Linville River. The farm was surrounded by a natural fortress of mountains—Grandmother Mountain to the east, Flat Rock to the southeast, Pixie Mountain to the west, and Moore Mountain to the northwest. To the north, Brier Knob rose like a silent guardian, and to the northeast, Emma's favorite, the grand Grandfather Mountain, stood tall above them all.

In this tranquil haven, tucked away in the heart of the Blue Ridge Mountains, the small community of Linville thrived, much like its Scottish roots—resilient, steeped in history, and at peace with nature. The seasons here painted the landscape in vivid strokes of color and texture, with spring's wildflowers giving way to the vibrant greens of summer, the deep oranges and reds of fall, and the quiet white stillness of winter. It was a place that seemed to breathe in time with its people, a refuge from the world.

Ryan spent five years of retirement fly-fishing the Linville River, savoring the quiet rhythm of casting his line into the cool, clear waters. Between fishing trips, he tended to the farm, finding satisfaction in the simple tasks that marked each day. But his time in this peaceful place was cut short by an untimely heart attack. Three years have passed since his death, but for Erin, it still feels as though the wound is fresh. Her memories of Ryan linger like the mist that often rises from the river—soft but ever-present, a quiet echo of the life they shared.

As Emma drove down W. Lenoir Street, memories of childhood visits to Mac's Convenience Store surfaced. Mac, a local institution, had run the store for over twenty-five years. Everyone knew him, and everyone loved his famous hot dogs. Emma's first visit had been at age eight, on Bring Your Daughter to Work Day, when her dad had taken her there for lunch. The memory always made her smile. Mac's, a large white building with a neon red cursive sign, was tucked on the corner of S. Saunders and W. Lenoir. The place had a timeless quality about it. Though the building was old and the paint worn, it always looked tidy and fresh. No trash littered the parking lot, and the black asphalt was pristine. School buses from local field trips frequently stopped by to grab snacks when visiting the North Carolina Museum of Natural Sciences or the State Capitol.

Mac and Ryan had been college buddies, both attending North Carolina State and later serving together for four years in the 82nd Airborne at Fort Bragg. They'd jumped out of airplanes all over the world during their tour of duty, and their stories were legendary. Though both men had no siblings, they were brothers in spirit. Mac was like an uncle to Emma, always there with a kind word or a lesson about life. Now in his late fifties and widowed, Mac had grown children who lived busy lives. He cherished the company of visitors, especially the school children who passed through his doors. "None better in town," Mac always said about his hot dogs. "Not even Costco's!"

Parking on the south side of the building—just as her dad always had—Emma stepped out of her patrol car. "The spaces out front are for customers," he used to say. She smiled, remembering those small moments with him.

As she entered the store, she spotted Mac sweeping the floor. "No help today?" Emma asked, planting a kiss on his smooth brown cheek.

"No, darlin', just me and this broom today," Mac replied, his eyes twinkling. "You've been busy, though." He eyed the dry fly she pinned to his apron—a new addition for his collection.

"You've got to use the right fly for the season," Emma grinned. "Hey, when are you coming fishing with me?"

Mac chuckled. "As soon as I can get some reliable help around here. Where's Dave?"

"Dentist appointment," Emma said, heading toward the beverage coolers. "We're meeting here for lunch afterward." She paused to glance at the North Carolina fishing chart on the wall, then turned the corner toward the ladies' room.

The bell above the door jingled as Emma disappeared into the restroom. A young man, likely in his late teens, walked into the store. Mac looked up from sweeping the floor. "What can I help you with, son?"

The young man pulled a gun from beneath his T-shirt, pointing it at Mac. "Give me all the money in the register."

Mac's expression remained calm, though his voice was firm. "Son, you don't want to do this. How much do you need?"

Before the young man could answer, a second man burst into the store, erratic and panicked. "What's taking so long?" he shouted at the first gunman. Spotting Mac, the second man pulled out a gun and fired twice, hitting him in the chest.

Emma, just emerging from the restroom, froze. The first gunman turned toward her, his eyes narrowing. Without a chance to react, Emma was struck twice. Both Mac and Emma collapsed to the floor as the robbers fled, their footsteps echoing in the silence that followed.

Minutes later, Jimmy—never one to be first at anything—was the first to reach the scene. He gasped as he saw a police officer lying in a pool of blood. Panicked, he rushed to her, checking for a pulse. It was faint, but it was there. Grabbing the radio microphone clipped to her vest, Jimmy pressed the button. "Hello? Hello? Can anyone hear me? A lady officer has been shot." The radio crackled, then went silent.

Then one voice cut through the static, sharp and urgent. "Who is this?"

"I'm at Mac's," Jimmy gasped, barely able to catch his breath. "Mac's been shot, and so has the officer. It's bad. It's real bad.

7

Please hurry!" He dropped the microphone, stumbling toward the counter where Mac lay on the floor, the broom still clutched in his hand. His heart sank as he found no pulse. "Mac was the kindest man I've ever known," Jimmy whispered, tears welling in his eyes. He wiped them away, stepping toward the door, just as he heard the sirens approaching. "This is a sad day. A very sad day," he muttered under his breath, waiting for the police and ambulance to arrive.

Chapter 2

Not Just a Partner

Jimmy sat on a weathered bench in Lenoir Street Park, the rough wood pressing against the back of his thighs as he flipped through the dog-eared pages of a paperback he'd just picked up at the used bookstore down the street. The scent of old paper mixed with the faint aroma of cut grass and distant car exhaust, a strange but familiar city blend. Overhead, the trees whispered to each other, their leaves rustling in the light afternoon breeze.

A sharp pop shattered the stillness.

Jimmy froze, his pulse spiking. A car backfire, maybe?

A second crack followed—louder, sharper, reverberating through the park like a snapped bone. A chill crawled up his spine. That wasn't a car.

The noise had come from the direction of Mac's, the corner store where he often grabbed a bite after browsing for books. His stomach growled, but hunger took a back seat to the cold grip of unease in his chest. If he was wrong, no harm—he'd still get a hot dog. If he was right... well, he didn't want to think about that yet.

He shoved the book into his jacket pocket, stood, and brushed off his jeans. The rough fabric scraped against his palms, grounding him. His feet carried him forward before his mind caught up, drawn by an instinct he couldn't ignore.

As he rounded the corner, the screech of tires cut through the air like a blade. A blue sedan roared past, its taillights flashing red as it vanished down Lenoir Street. For a split second, Jimmy caught a glimpse of the driver—broad shoulders, a shadowed face. Someone else sat in the passenger seat, but before he could make out any details, they were gone.

The metallic tang of blood hit him the second he stepped inside Mac's. The bell above the door jingled weakly, absurdly out of place against the horror before him. Two bodies lay crumpled on the floor, their blood seeping into the worn linoleum, glistening under the fluorescent lights. A carton of milk had tipped over near the counter, a white river spilling toward the red.

His breath hitched. His pulse thundered in his ears.

"That's what I heard—two quick shots, then a whole bunch all at once," he told the officers minutes later, his voice steady despite the way his hands shook at his sides. "I saw a blue car speeding away, but I couldn't see how many people were inside—at least two in the front."

A soft, ragged gasp pulled his attention toward the paramedics working frantically nearby.

Emma.

She lay on the floor, a paramedic securing an oxygen mask over her mouth. Her chest rose and fell in shallow, uneven bursts, her uniform soaked through with blood. Every breath she took was a battle, her face contorted in pain. The cool air filling her lungs barely reached past the burning ache spreading through her ribs. She tried to speak, to say something—Mac's name, maybe—but no words came.

Voices blurred. Lights smeared into bright, unfocused halos above her. Then came the unmistakable jolt of being lifted onto a gurney, straps tightening across her body.

"We've got her," a voice said, firm and certain.

The world tilted. The ceiling of Mac's receded as they wheeled her outside.

Dave's tires screamed against the pavement as he pulled into the parking lot, his heart hammering against his ribs. He barely threw the car into Park before bolting out, his boots pounding against the asphalt.

The moment he saw the gurney and saw *her*, the breath was knocked from his chest.

Emma.

Blood streaked her uniform, her face pale beneath the oxygen mask. She was too still. Too quiet.

"What happened?" he demanded, his voice sharp enough to cut.

A reporter, barely glancing up from their notepad, muttered, "Two people shot. One's a female officer."

Female officer.

Dave didn't care about the other details. He was already moving, pushing past the small cluster of bystanders and flashing lights, straight to her side.

"She's 24, allergic to penicillin," he barked to the paramedic, the words automatic—drilled into him through years of partnership. But his voice was tight, barely controlled.

"Copy that—24, allergic to penicillin," the paramedic relayed into the radio as the ambulance doors slammed shut.

Dave barely hesitated before climbing in after them.

The sirens wailed as they sped toward UNC REX Hospital, but all Dave could hear was the sound of Emma's breathing— shallow, strained, too weak. He wanted to say something, to tell her to hold on, but the words felt useless. Instead, he gripped the edge of the gurney, his knuckles white, as the paramedics worked around him, their voices clipped and urgent.

As soon as they pulled into the emergency bay, the doors flew open. The trauma team was already there, waiting.

"We've got her," a nurse said, her tone brisk and confident.

Dave jumped down from the ambulance, his legs unsteady, but as he moved to follow, another nurse blocked his path.

"You can't go in there."

"She's my partner," Dave said, but the words felt too small for what he meant.

The nurse's expression softened. "Wait in the lounge. We'll update you when she's out of surgery."

Dave took a step back, running a hand over his face. Sweat clung to his skin. His mouth was dry, his throat tight.

She's my partner.

But she was more than that.

With shaking fingers, he pulled out his phone. Scrolling through his contacts, he stopped at *Erin Patterson*. He hesitated only a second before hitting call.

The line barely rang twice before Erin's voice came through, laced with concern.

"Dave? What's wrong? Is everything all right? You sound—"

"It's Emma," he interrupted, his voice breaking despite his effort to hold it together. "She... she's been shot."

The sharp inhale on the other end was like a knife to his chest.

"Shot?" Erin's voice trembled. "Oh my God, no... Emma? Where is she? Is she—"

"She's alive," he said quickly. "She's alive. She's in surgery right now at UNC REX. They're doing everything they can."

A shaky exhale. Then, panic.

"Surgery? How bad is it, Dave? Tell me the truth."

Dave swallowed hard. "It's bad, Erin. She was hit twice, but they got her here fast. The doctors say that makes a difference. She's strong—she's fighting."

A choked sob. "She's my baby, Dave. My baby girl... I thought I had more time before this kind of call."

Dave closed his eyes, guilt twisting in his gut. "I don't think she was fully conscious. She tried to speak, but... I don't know if she could."

Erin's voice shifted, raw and edged with something deeper—anger, fear, or grief. "I sat by her father's hospital bed after he was shot, wondering if I'd lose him. And now, it's her."

"I know, Erin," Dave said quietly. "And I'm so sorry. I should've been with her."

A beat of silence. Then, softer—still pained, but steady. "Don't do that to yourself, Dave. You and Emma... you look out for each other. But that doesn't stop the fear."

Dave exhaled slowly, nodding. "I know. But Emma's alive. And we're going to get her through this."

Erin sniffled, gathering herself. "I'll be there soon. Tell her I love her. And Dave..."

He braced himself.

"Promise me you won't leave her alone."

His throat tightened. "I promise. I'm not going anywhere."

And he meant it.

Because Emma wasn't just his partner. She was the one person he couldn't afford to lose.

Chapter 3

Waiting and Recovery

Dave's boots scuffed against the speckled linoleum floor as he paced the waiting room, his phone pressed tightly against his ear. The faint scent of disinfectant and stale coffee clung to the air, mixing with the sterile chill that seemed to seep into his bones. The waiting area was filled with the muted hum of whispered conversations, the occasional squeak of chairs, and the soft rustling of officers shifting in their seats.

"Emma has been in surgery for five hours, and her status hasn't changed on the board," he muttered into his phone, glancing at the glowing red text on the monitor that still read *In Surgery*. His voice carried a blend of weariness and determination as he addressed Chief Williams. "Yes, Chief, I'll call you as soon as I hear something. No, there's no need to cut your conference short. Emma's strong—she's going to pull through, but I have to go now."

He ended the call abruptly, not because he wanted to, but because his heart was heavy with the weight of uncertainty.

His throat felt dry, the lingering taste of burnt hospital coffee doing little to soothe the tightness there. He swallowed hard and turned toward the couch where two women sat, their faces etched with exhaustion and fear.

Erin Patterson, Emma's mother, gripped a balled-up tissue so tightly in her hand that her knuckles had turned white. At 49, she was still sharp, still fierce, but tonight she looked small beneath the fluorescent hospital lighting, the streaks of gray in her auburn hair more pronounced. Beside her, Kate Campbell, a longtime family friend, sat with her hands folded in her lap, her own worry etched deep in the lines around her mouth.

"Any update on Emma?" Erin asked, her voice barely above a whisper.

"Not yet," Dave replied, kneeling beside her and meeting her gaze. There was an ache behind her eyes, the kind that comes from years of waiting for bad news. "But I'm keeping close tabs on her progress. Is there anything I can get you?"

Before Erin could respond, Kate stood, smoothing the wrinkles from her sweater. "I'll grab us some coffee," she offered, disappearing down the hallway.

The silence between them stretched, heavy and suffocating. The quiet murmur of conversations among the other officers did nothing to ease the pressure building in Dave's chest.

Erin reached for his hand, her fingers cold and trembling. "You've seen situations like this before," she said, searching his face for reassurance. "Tell me, Dave. Tell me Emma can make it through this."

Dave's throat tightened. He had been in situations like this before, but none of them had involved Emma. His partner. His best friend. The person he'd spent years pretending he didn't feel more for than he should. The idea of a world without her—without her sharp wit, her fire, her unwavering strength—was unbearable.

"Of course she will," he said firmly, squeezing Erin's hand. "The paramedics got to her quickly, and the surgeons here are the best. Emma is strong—stronger than anyone I know. She'll pull through."

Erin nodded, but her lips trembled as she blinked back tears. "Pray the Lord's Prayer with me, Dave," she whispered.

Dave bowed his head, his fingers still wrapped around hers. His voice was steady, but his heart clenched with every word.

"Our Father, who art in heaven…"

The words came easily, but his mind kept circling back to Emma. The last time they'd prayed together was over a suspect who hadn't made it—one of those moments that had left a mark neither of them talked about. But this was different. This was her.

Their prayer was interrupted by the soft voice of Nurse Franklin.

"Mrs. Patterson?"

Erin looked up, her breath catching.

"Emma is out of surgery," the nurse said with a reassuring smile. "She's in recovery now. Once she's fully awake, we'll move her to a room where you can see her."

Erin's shoulders sagged with relief as she closed her eyes, her lips moving soundlessly in prayer. When she looked up again, tears spilled freely down her cheeks. "Praise God," she whispered, her voice cracking.

Kate returned just in time to hear the news, setting down two cups of coffee before embracing Erin tightly. "Our Emma made it," she murmured.

Dave exhaled slowly, pulling out his phone to update the chief. "Chief Williams, Emma is out of surgery and in recovery. I'll let you know more as soon as we can see her," he said, his voice steadier now, though the tension in his shoulders hadn't eased.

Around the waiting room, officers who had been watching the surgical status board saw the status change to *In Recovery*. The room seemed to exhale collectively, relief spreading through the space like a wave.

Dave turned back to Erin and Kate. "Everyone's pulling for Emma," he said softly.

When Erin smiled faintly in return, he slipped away.

***

The hallway leading to Recovery was quieter, the sounds of the hospital softened but were ever-present. The rhythmic beeping of monitors drifted through half-closed doors, the steady squeak of nurses' shoes breaking the hush. The air was thick with the antiseptic scent of alcohol wipes and sterilized equipment, but beneath it was something else—the lingering coppery tang of blood, a grim reminder of why Emma was here in the first place.

Dave approached the desk, his badge still clipped to his belt. A nurse glanced up and immediately recognized him.

"You're here for Emma Patterson?"

He nodded.

"She's stable, but still sedated. You can go in for a few minutes," she said, motioning toward the door.

"Thank you," Dave murmured, his voice thick with gratitude.

The room was dimly lit, a single monitor beeping steadily in the corner. Emma lay still, her face pale against the stark whiteness of the hospital sheets. Her auburn hair fanned across the pillow, its usual fire muted but still vivid to him. He hesitated at the door, his chest tightening at the sight of her so vulnerable.

He had never seen her like this.

For years, Emma had been the strongest person in the room. The one who never backed down from a fight, never hesitated to put herself in danger if it meant protecting someone else. But now, the woman lying in front of him wasn't the fierce officer who had his back in every firefight. She was just Emma. And for the first time, he allowed himself to admit how much that meant.

Slowly, he stepped closer, pulling up a chair beside her bed. He reached for her hand, careful not to disturb the IV line, and held it gently.

"You gave us a scare, Em," he said softly. "But you're going to be okay. You've got a whole army out there pulling for you."

His throat tightened as his eyes searched her face, hoping for any flicker of recognition. Her breathing was steady but shallow, her lashes dark against her pale skin.

After a moment, he leaned forward, his voice low but steady. "I'm going to read something to you. Something that makes me think of you."

He pulled out his phone and found the words, his voice barely above a whisper as he began:

> "Ae fond kiss, and then we sever;
> Ae farewell, and then forever!
> Deep in heart-wrung tears I'll pledge thee,
> Warring sighs and groans I'll wage thee.
> Who shall say that Fortune grieves him,
> Me, nae cheerful' twinkle lights me;
> Dark despair around benights me.
>
> I'll ne'er blame my partial fancy,
> Naething could resist my Emma;
> But to see her was to love her;
> Love but her, and love forever.
> Had we never lov'd sae kindly,
> Had we never lov'd sae blindly,
> Never met – or never parted-
> We had ne'er been broken-hearted."

His voice wavered as he substituted her name for the original.

A nurse entered quietly, pausing in the doorway. She listened for a moment, her head tilting as she recognized the words.

"Is that Robert Burns?" she asked softly, not wanting to disturb him.

Dave looked up, startled, then nodded. "It is," he said simply.

"It's beautiful," the nurse replied with a small smile before slipping away.

Dave turned back to Emma, his hand still wrapped around hers. "You've got to come back to us, Emma," he whispered. "There's too much left for you to do. Too many people who need you."

The steady beeping of the monitor was the only response, but Dave stayed, holding her hand as he quietly finished the poem.

And for the first time in a long time, he allowed himself to feel just how much he needed her too.

Chapter 4

Fishing and News

Emma floated on the edge of consciousness, her body heavy, her mind adrift. Pain rippled through her like an undertow, pulling her deeper into the past. A memory unspooled, vivid and sharp, like sunlight reflecting on a river's surface.

It was spring—April—just before Easter and just before her first Holy Communion. She was seven years old, standing on the rocky bank of the family farm's river, her fly rod clutched tightly in her hands. The air was alive with the hum of insects and the scent of blooming dogwood. The water babbled as if it, too, had secrets to tell. The crisp scent of pine mixed with the earthy aroma of damp soil, a fragrance so familiar it felt like home.

"Hey, Emma," Mac called out, wading knee-deep in the stream beside her dad. His voice was warm, gruff, but full of humor, like gravel softened by years of storytelling. "Your dad says the big day's next Sunday. Are you ready?"

Emma squinted up at him, the sun warming her face. "I think so. I have confession first, though. I have to get ready for that." She pulled a new fly from her tackle box, her small fingers nimble as she tied it to her line, the silk thread cool against her fingertips. At seven years old, she was already her father's fishing protégé.

Mac chuckled, casting his line with an effortless flick of his wrist. "We don't have confession where I go to church. Baptists don't do that."

Emma paused, curious. "Why not?"

"Don't need a priest for forgiveness," Mac explained, reeling in his line just enough to feel the tug of the current. "But I'll tell you something—sometimes sin weighs on you, no matter what. Having someone say, 'You're forgiven,' that could help a lot of folks."

Her dad, Ryan, snorted from farther upstream. "Mac, don't go putting ideas in her head. Next thing you know, she'll be confessing her 'sins' every time she loses a fish."

Emma grinned. "Maybe I'll confess that I catch more fish than you two."

As if on cue, Mac's line jerked. He leaned back, reeling in a lively trout. The fish splashed, sending cool droplets of water into the air, the scent of river mud and fresh fish mingling around them. "Looks like this one's going in the creel," he said, holding it up for them to see.

"Nice keeper," Emma said, eyes sparkling. "At least eight inches."

"Nine, if not ten," Mac teased, unhooking the fish and slipping it into his creel. "What do you think, Ryan?"

"I think the two of you are scaring off all the fish," Ryan said, sloshing over to them. He tousled Emma's hair, leaving her giggling. "C'mon, Tadpole. Get your feet wet if you want to catch something bigger than your ego."

Emma stuck her tongue out at him but waded into the cool water anyway, her boots sinking into the soft silt. Her father smiled, pride flickering in his eyes as he watched her cast her line with practiced precision.

"Who's ready for lunch?" Ryan called out, making his way to the ice chest near the pickup truck. The faint scent of smoked ham and freshly baked bread drifted from the cooler, mixing with the river's crisp air.

"What's for lunch, Dad?" Emma asked, climbing onto the riverbank. But before he could answer, the memory dissolved, slipping through her grasp like water through her fingers.

The present rushed back in jagged fragments. The sterile smell of antiseptic. The beep of distant monitors. A dull, aching throb that radiated through her body. Her throat felt raw, as though she had swallowed gravel, and the faint taste of iron lingered on her tongue.

She tried to open her eyes, but they felt too heavy. Her father's voice lingered in her mind, clear and steady. "Get your feet wet, Tadpole. You're stronger than you think."

Am I? she wondered. The darkness pulled her under again.

***

The steady beeping of the heart monitor anchored Erin Patterson to reality. She sat rigidly beside her daughter's hospital bed, fingers clenched in the fabric of the blanket covering

Emma. The air in the hospital room was thick with the sharp bite of disinfectant, so different from the fresh, open scent of Linville's mountains. The hum of machines mixed with the occasional murmur of nurses in the hall, creating an eerie symphony of controlled chaos.

Kate sat nearby, watching Emma's still form with a mix of fear and determination. "She looks so… small," Kate whispered, her voice barely audible over the machinery. "I've never seen her like this."

Erin nodded, swallowing past the lump in her throat. "She's always been strong... like her father."

The door creaked open, and Dr. Calloway stepped inside, his face carefully composed. A nurse followed, her shoes squeaking against the linoleum as she checked Emma's IV.

Dr. Calloway cleared his throat. "Mrs. Patterson, I have an update."

Erin straightened. "Go on."

"Emma sustained significant injuries. One of the bullets caused extensive damage to the artery supplying her left kidney. We did everything we could, but the damage was too severe. We had to remove it."

Erin's breath hitched. Kate reached over, gripping her hand.

"There's more," Dr. Calloway continued. "During testing, we discovered that Emma's right kidney is underdeveloped—renal hypoplasia. It means she'll need a transplant. We're already starting the donor matching process."

Erin's grip on Kate's hand tightened until her knuckles turned white. "And the other bullet?"

Dr. Calloway exhaled. "It missed her heart by millimeters. It was a close call."

The words felt like a punch to the gut. Erin closed her eyes, willing herself to stay composed. "She's alive," she murmured, as if saying it aloud would make it feel more real.

A faint movement drew their attention. Emma's fingers twitched, her eyelids fluttering. A weak sound escaped her lips— "Mom?"

Erin was at her side in an instant. "I'm here, sweetheart."

Emma's eyes opened sluggishly, her gaze unfocused. She tried to speak, but her throat was dry. "Water..."

Kate grabbed a cup, guiding the straw to Emma's lips. She took a small sip, wincing at the effort.

"What... happened?" Emma whispered.

Erin brushed stray strands of hair from her daughter's forehead. "You were hurt, but you're safe now. You'll need time to heal."

Emma's eyes flickered with understanding. "Mac?"

Erin hesitated, but the sorrow in her gaze was answer enough. Emma turned her head away, blinking rapidly. A tear slipped down her cheek, and Erin gently wiped it away.

"We'll get through this, Emma," Erin whispered, voice thick with emotion. "You're strong and a fighter like your dad."

Emma squeezed her mother's hand, her grip weak but present. "I hope so."

Kate leaned in. "When you're ready, we'll hit the Linville River again. Just like old times." She forced a grin. "Only this time, you're catching fish with your bare hands."

A ghost of a smile crossed Emma's lips. "Deal."

For the first time since the shooting, hope flickered in her chest. The road ahead was long, but she wasn't walking it alone.

Chapter 5

Support and the Search is Over

The news of Emma's need for a kidney transplant spread quickly through her close circle of family, friends, and fellow officers. Each person—without hesitation—stepped forward, eager to be tested to see if they could be the one to save her life. The outpouring of support left Erin and Kate humbled, but Emma, still grappling with the reality of her situation, struggled to express the overwhelming gratitude she felt.

Dave was the first to volunteer. "I'll do it," he said firmly during a quiet moment in Emma's hospital room. His voice, steady and low, carried the unwavering resolve of a man determined to do whatever it took. The dim hospital light cast shadows along his strong jawline, his tired eyes darkened with worry. "I'll get tested first thing tomorrow."

Emma, propped against a mound of pillows, turned her head toward him. The crisp scent of antiseptic filled the air, battling with the stale remnants of hospital food. She was exhausted, pain lacing through her body with each shallow breath, but she found the strength to meet his gaze. "Dave, you don't have to—"

"I want to." His voice softened, and he leaned forward, elbows resting on his knees. "You think I'd sit back and do nothing? I couldn't live with myself if I didn't try."

Kate, sitting on the edge of Emma's bed, placed a warm hand over her forearm. "Me too," she added, her tone softer but no less determined. "You've been my best friend since we were kids. There's nothing I wouldn't do for you."

Emma's throat tightened. The words, the sheer depth of their love and loyalty, made it hard to swallow past the lump that formed. "I'm lucky to have you both. But... it's a lot to ask."

Dave shook his head. "It's not a lot. It's what you do for family, Emma. And you're family."

Kate nodded. "And for friends," she added with a small smile. "Especially ones who taught me how to fish and how to sneak cookies from the kitchen without getting caught."

The next few days passed in a blur of hospital visits, medical appointments, and tests. Officers from the precinct formed a line, ready to give their blood and hoping for a match. Even Chief Williams showed up, rolling up his sleeves with a wry grin. "It's the least I can do," he said.

Erin watched the flood of support with a heart full of gratitude. "Emma has always been surrounded by good people," she told Kate one evening as they sat together in the hospital's family room. "But seeing it firsthand like this? It's overwhelming."

Kate reached over and squeezed Erin's hand. "She's easy to love. And she's a fighter, Erin. Just like you."

Finally, after what felt like an eternity of waiting, Dr. Calloway called Erin, Kate, and Dave into a small conference room. His expression was calm but unreadable as he placed a folder on the table and folded his hands.

"We've completed the compatibility testing," he began, glancing at each of them in turn. "I'm pleased to share that we've found a match."

Erin's hand flew to her chest. Dave leaned forward, his brow furrowed with both hope and anticipation. Kate's grip on her coffee cup tightened.

"It's you, Ms. Campbell," Dr. Calloway said, his gaze settling on Kate. "Your results show a very high level of compatibility with Emma. You're an excellent candidate for donation."

For a moment, the room was silent. Then Kate let out a breath she hadn't realized she was holding. "It's me?" she repeated, her voice trembling with equal parts relief and disbelief.

Dr. Calloway nodded. "Yes. If you're willing to proceed, we can begin preparing for the surgery immediately. The sooner we act, the better for Emma."

Kate's answer was immediate. "Of course I'll do it," she said, her voice steady now. "When can we start?"

When they returned to Emma's room, Kate couldn't contain her excitement. She sat down beside her best friend, a bright smile lighting her face. "Guess what, Emma?" she said, taking Emma's hand in hers.

Emma's eyes, though weary, searched Kate's face. "What?" she asked, her voice barely above a whisper.

"I'm your match," Kate said, her voice brimming with joy. "I'm going to give you my kidney. We're a perfect fit."

For a moment, Emma was too stunned to speak. Then her lips trembled, and tears spilled down her cheeks. "Kate," she whispered. "You'd do that for me?"

Kate's grin widened. "Of course I would. You're my best friend. And besides, I owe you one after you pulled me out of the river that summer."

Emma let out a shaky laugh, the sound a mix of relief and gratitude. "I don't know how to thank you."

"You don't have to," Kate said gently. "Just get better. That's all I need."

As Dave stood back, watching Emma and Kate, a quiet relief settled over him. He had been prepared to do whatever it took, but knowing Emma had a match lifted a weight from his shoulders. Yet, there was something else—something deeper—that he hadn't yet allowed himself to name. He stepped closer, his voice gentle. "Emma, you scared the heck out of us."

Emma turned her tired eyes toward him, offering a small, teasing smirk. "You too?"

Dave chuckled, the warmth of it settling in his chest. "Yeah. Me too." He reached out, squeezing her hand. "I'm glad you're getting what you need."

She squeezed back, her touch weak but certain. "Me too."

And in that moment, unspoken between them was something fragile but growing. Something that neither of them was quite ready to name—but it was there, steady as a heartbeat.

***

In the days leading up to the surgery, Emma's hospital room became a hub of warmth and energy, a stark contrast to the sterile white walls and the faint scent of antiseptic that lingered in the air. The soft hum of the medical monitors blended with bursts of laughter, the rustle of jackets as visitors came and went, and the occasional chime of a heart monitor, a steady reminder of the fight ahead.

The officers from the precinct showed up in shifts, their presence a testament to the bond they all shared. They brought with them the scent of freshly brewed coffee from the station, still warm in their hands, and boxes of donuts—though most of them sat untouched, their sugary aroma mingling with the sharper hospital air.

"Didn't think I'd see you laid up like this, Patterson," Officer Morales teased, tossing a small, stuffed bear onto Emma's bed. The fabric was soft against her fingertips, its newness contrasting the rough hospital sheets beneath her hands.

Emma smirked. "Yeah, well, even the toughest need a break sometimes."

"Darn right," Officer Jenkins chimed in, his voice deep but gentle. "And when you get back, don't think you're skipping out on training rookies. No one gives them training like you do."

Emma rolled her eyes, but her chest ached with gratitude. These were her people—her second family.

A prayer circle formed on the eve of the surgery. Hands linked, the room hushed, save for the soft shuffle of feet against the polished linoleum floor and the occasional sniffle of someone fighting back emotion. Chief Williams led the prayer, his voice gravelly yet steady, filling the room with a quiet strength.

"We ask for protection over Emma and Kate," he said, the words wrapping around them like a shield. "For steady hands in the operating room, for strength in recovery, and for the blessing of friendship that has already proven to be a miracle in itself."

Emma squeezed Kate's hand, feeling the warmth and steadiness of her best friend's grip. She inhaled deeply, catching a hint of Kate's familiar vanilla-scented lotion—something grounding in the whirlwind of uncertainty.

Finally, the day of the surgery arrived. The morning light filtered through the half-drawn blinds, casting soft golden streaks across the white-tiled floor. The room smelled faintly of the breakfast she hadn't been allowed to eat—scrambled eggs and toast, carried past her door on a nurse's tray, the phantom scent teasing her empty stomach.

Kate stood beside her bed, dressed in a loose hospital gown that swayed slightly with her movements. Her long hair had been pulled back into a loose braid, stray wisps curling around her face.

"You ready for this?" Kate asked, her voice light, but her deep brown eyes betrayed the weight of the moment.

Emma swallowed, her throat dry, the taste of the ice chips from earlier still lingering on her tongue. "Ready as I'll ever be."

Kate leaned down, wrapping her in a tight embrace. Emma felt the cool fabric of the hospital gown against her cheek, the steady rise and fall of Kate's breathing, and the way her arms held on just a little longer than usual.

"I'll see you on the other side, bestie," Kate murmured. Then she pulled back, a smirk breaking through the seriousness. "And when this is over, we're celebrating. With cookies. Lots of cookies."

Emma managed a small smile, the corners of her lips trembling. "Deal."

The door creaked open, and Dr. Calloway stepped inside, his presence calm, his blue scrubs crisp and professional. He smelled of soap and something faintly medicinal, a reassuring yet clinical scent.

"It's time," he said gently, his voice carrying an authority that made the reality sink in.

Kate was wheeled toward the door, but just before disappearing into the hallway, she looked back. Her fingers lifted in a thumbs-up, her expression a mixture of excitement and determination.

"We've got this," she called out.

Emma watched her go, blinking against the sting of tears. She closed her eyes, exhaling slowly, and in the quiet, her father's voice whispered through her memory.

"Get your feet wet, Tadpole. You're stronger than you think."

And for the first time in weeks, Emma believed it.

Chapter 6

Waiting and Remembrance

The waiting room pulsed with a restless quiet, an uneasy stillness broken only by the rhythmic ticking of the clock mounted high on the sterile white wall. The air was thick with the scent of antiseptic, masking the faint traces of stale coffee and floor polish. Fluorescent lighting buzzed softly overhead, casting a cold glow over the rows of stiff-backed chairs lined against the walls.

Daniel Campbell sat in one corner, his broad hands clasped tightly together, knuckles pale with tension. A man who had spent a lifetime forging himself in fire—through heartbreak, loss, and hard-earned resilience—he had long since learned to wear his strength like armor. But tonight, that armor felt brittle.

Across the room, Erin Patterson sat stiffly, her arms crossed over her chest as though trying to physically hold herself together. Her gaze flicked up to the clock every few minutes, her lips moving in a silent prayer, though the words never fully formed. She had always been beautiful in a quiet way—effortlessly so. Even now, with exhaustion hollowing her features and worry etched into every line of her face, Daniel couldn't help but notice the soft curve of her jaw, the way her dark auburn hair had come loose from the bun on the nape of her neck.

He let out a breath, shifting slightly in his seat. The room smelled faintly of industrial-strength cleaner, but beneath it, he caught a trace of something familiar—lavender and chamomile, Yardley English Lavender. Erin's scent. He remembered it from years ago in high school, the way it used to linger on his hoodie when she borrowed it on cool autumn nights.

He cleared his throat. "How are you holding up, Erin?"

She startled slightly, pulled from her thoughts. For a second, something flickered in her expression—surprise, maybe even something softer—but it disappeared as quickly as it had come. She forced a faint smile. "I'm all right. Just… anxious. I hate not knowing."

Daniel nodded. "It's the waiting that gets to you." His voice was steady, but there was an edge to it—one that only came from experience. "But they're in good hands. Kate's tough. Just like her mom was."

At the mention of Elizabeth, something tightened in Daniel's chest. The memory of his late wife was a constant, lingering just beneath the surface of his thoughts. Her vivacious smile, the sound of her laughter, the way her hands had always been warm no matter the season. He swallowed hard and looked away, his gaze settling on the untouched coffee cup sitting on the table in front of him.

Erin's voice was softer when she spoke again. "You miss her, don't you?"

Daniel let out a slow exhale. "Every day," he admitted. His voice was low, rough like gravel. "She was the best of us. Strong, steady... made life feel easier, even when it wasn't."

A long silence stretched between them. Then Erin said quietly, "You've done a wonderful job with Kate. She's a remarkable woman."

Daniel huffed a soft laugh. "That's all her," he said, shaking his head. "She's got her mother's heart and stubbornness. And a bit of her dad's temper, I suppose."

Erin let out a chuckle, the sound light but tinged with something wistful. It had been a long time since they had laughed together. The realization made Daniel's chest ache.

"You give yourself too little credit," she murmured. "Kate's brave. She didn't hesitate to step up for Emma."

Daniel's gaze met hers, and for a fleeting moment, the years between them seemed to fall away. The weight of time, of past choices, of heartbreak—it all still existed, but in this moment, it felt distant.

He wanted to say something. Something about the past, about the choices they had made, about the way he had loved her once—and, if he was honest with himself, the way he still did. But the words wouldn't come.

Instead, he shifted in his seat and glanced toward the hallway that led to the operating rooms. "It's strange, isn't it?" he mused, his voice quiet. "How life pulls us back together when we least expect it."

Erin tilted her head slightly, studying him. "Life has a way of doing that," she murmured. "But it doesn't erase what's already happened."

Daniel nodded slowly, the unspoken meaning of her words sinking in. "No, it doesn't. But it doesn't mean we can't move forward either."

Before Erin could respond, the doors to the waiting room swung open. Nurse Franklin stepped inside, her calm, measured steps cutting through the thick tension in the air.

"Mrs. Patterson, Mr. Campbell," she said gently. "I wanted to give you an update. The surgeries went well. Emma is stable and recovering as expected."

Erin let out a shuddering breath, her hands flying to cover her mouth as tears welled in her eyes. "Thank God," she whispered.

Daniel stood, his breath escaping in a long, heavy sigh, the tension in his chest loosening for the first time all day. "And Kate?" he asked, his voice steady but lined with a father's worry.

"She's stable," Nurse Franklin assured him. "Still asleep, but doing well. You'll be able to see her in a few hours."

Erin reached out without thinking, her fingers gripping Daniel's hand. Her touch was warm, her skin soft against his own roughened palm. "Thank you for being here," she murmured, her voice thick with emotion.

Daniel's fingers tightened around hers for just a moment. "Of course," he said softly. "I wouldn't be anywhere else."

As the nurse left, Erin wiped at her tears, and Daniel let go of her hand, though he already missed the warmth of it.

The waiting room had mostly emptied out now, leaving just the two of them. Outside, the sky had darkened, rain tapping softly against the windowpanes. The scent of freshly mopped floors mingled with the lingering aroma of the vending machine's stale popcorn.

Daniel let out a breath and leaned back in his chair. His thoughts drifted to The Stag & Thistle, the pub he had built from the ground up after Elizabeth passed. He could almost hear the clink of glasses behind the bar, the low murmur of conversation, and the rich smell of oak wood and spiced whiskey filling the air.

"You know," he mused after a while, "when I first opened the pub, I thought it would just be a job—something to keep me busy after Elizabeth was gone. But it's more than that now. It's home."

Erin turned to him, curiosity flickering in her tired eyes. "Kate talks about it all the time," she said softly.

Daniel smiled faintly. "She's the heart of that place. She's the reason it feels alive. And I think... I think she's the reason I've kept going."

Erin nodded, understanding the weight of his words. "Our children have a way of grounding us, don't they?"

"They do," Daniel agreed. "And they remind us what really matters."

The two of them sat in silence for a while, their thoughts heavy but not unwelcome. Daniel found himself hoping—against all odds—that this moment of shared relief might be the first step toward something more.

For now, though, he was content to sit beside Erin, the ghosts of their past lingering in the space between them, waiting for whatever came next.

And maybe—just maybe—there was still time to find their way back to each other.

Chapter 7

Threads of Healing

The warm amber hues of the setting sun filtered through the hospital blinds, casting long golden streaks across the sterile white walls of Emma's room. The scent of antiseptic lingered in the air, mingling with the faint aroma of lavender from the lotion Erin had rubbed into Emma's hands earlier. The steady hum of the monitors provided a rhythmic backdrop, punctuated by the occasional beep—each sound a quiet reassurance that life carried on.

Emma stirred, her lashes fluttering against pale cheeks, the sensation of stiff sheets beneath her unfamiliar. A distant taste of metal lingered in her mouth, a reminder of the IV fluids keeping her hydrated. Her fingers curled slightly, brushing against the soft fabric of the blanket tucked around her. Slowly, her eyes opened to the dimly lit room, where her mother sat beside her, lost in thought, worry creased into her features.

"Mom?" Emma's voice was faint but steady, carrying the weight of exhaustion.

Erin snapped out of her reverie, her gaze immediately softening. Relief swept over her like a tide, the tension in her shoulders loosening as she leaned forward, instinctively brushing a stray strand of hair from Emma's forehead.

"I'm here, sweetheart," she murmured, her voice thick with emotion. Her touch was warm and comforting. "How are you feeling?"

Emma blinked, letting the question settle as she took a slow, deep breath. Her chest ached dully, her limbs heavy. "Tired... but okay," she admitted, her voice holding only a shadow of its usual strength. A brief pause, then "How's Kate?"

"She's doing well," Erin reassured her, squeezing her hand lightly. "She's in her room, resting. She was incredible, Emma. She never hesitated—not once."

Emma let out a small breath, her lips curving into a tired smile. "Of course, she didn't. That's Kate for you." Her smile faded slightly as her gaze drifted toward the window, where streaks of deep orange and violet painted the sky. Her brow furrowed. "Mom... how long was I out?"

Erin hesitated, carefully choosing her words. "A little over 24 hours since the surgery," she said gently. "But you're doing great. The doctors are really pleased with your progress."

Emma nodded slowly, her mind wading through the lingering haze of medication and exhaustion. She swallowed, her throat dry, the taste of saline still present. Her voice softened as she asked, "Mom, did anyone... else get hurt? At Mac's?"

The question hung in the air like a fragile thread, and Erin felt her chest tighten. She had known this moment would come, but facing it was another matter entirely. She reached for Emma's hand, clasping it tightly, feeling the delicate pulse beneath her fingertips.

"Emma, right now, I want you to focus on healing," Erin began gently, her voice steady but laced with emotion. "There's time to talk about everything else later."

Emma's eyes searched her mother's face, sensing the weight behind her words. The air between them carried the unspoken truth—something had happened, something Erin wasn't ready to say. Emma pressed her lips together, then nodded slowly. "Okay," she whispered, though the unease in her gaze lingered.

***

Across the hall, the same sunset bathed Kate's hospital room in hues of burnt orange and soft purple. The smell of disinfectant still lingered, though beneath it, the scent of the Earl Grey tea someone had left untouched on the bedside table added a hint of warmth. Kate lay against the pillows, her gaze fixed on the shifting sky outside.

A soft knock at the door pulled her attention. When it opened, Daniel stepped inside, his presence solid and familiar.

"Hey, Dad," Kate greeted him with a small but genuine smile.

Daniel crossed the room, his large frame moving carefully, as though the air around them was as fragile as glass. The chair beside her bed groaned slightly as he settled into it, reaching for her hand. His grip was warm and steady—anchoring.

45

"Hey, kiddo. How are you holding up?" he asked, his voice low, roughened by the weight of the last twenty-four hours.

Kate shrugged lightly, wincing at the movement. A playful glint flashed in her tired eyes. "You know me. Tough as nails."

Daniel chuckled, the sound deep and familiar. "That you are," he agreed, squeezing her hand. "But even nails need to rest after being hammered." His expression grew more serious, his blue eyes searching hers. "I'm proud of you, Kate. What you did... it wasn't just brave—it was extraordinary."

Kate's cheeks flushed, and she looked down at their joined hands. "She's my best friend, Dad. She's practically my sister. I couldn't not do it."

"I know," Daniel said, his voice filled with quiet admiration. "And that's what makes you so special. You put your heart into everything—even when it's hard."

A beat of silence passed, filled only by the rhythmic beeping of the monitors. Finally, Kate broke it with a hesitant question. "Dad... do you think Emma's going to be okay? Not just physically... but everything else?"

Daniel exhaled slowly, rubbing a hand over his beard. "She's been through a lot, that's for sure. But Emma's strong—just like you. It might take time, but she'll find her way."

Kate nodded, though uncertainty still weighed on her. "I just... I don't know how to help her through everything. And I know there's more she hasn't talked about yet. I can see it in her eyes."

"You help her by being there," Daniel said simply. "That's what you've always done. And when she's ready, she'll talk. Just give her time."

Kate let out a slow breath, his words settling over her like a blanket. She still didn't know what the future held for Emma, but she was determined to be by her side every step of the way.

***

Later that evening, Erin returned to Emma's room to find her daughter dozing lightly, the soft rise and fall of her chest a quiet reassurance. She sank into the chair by the bed, exhaustion weighing her down like a heavy cloak. The scent of the hospital—disinfectant, latex, and the sterile chill of processed air—felt suffocating.

How would she tell Emma about Mac? How would she help her daughter find her footing again after everything that had happened?

The questions churned in her mind as she closed her eyes and whispered a quiet prayer. She prayed for guidance, for strength, and for the courage to face the challenges ahead. Most of all, she prayed for Emma's healing—not just of her body, but of her heart and soul.

Across the hall, Kate drifted off to sleep, her father still seated by her bedside, his fingers resting lightly over hers. And in the stillness of the night, the threads of their lives—woven together by love, loss, and resilience—held fast, carrying them toward whatever lay ahead.

Chapter 8

Aftermath

The gentle rhythm of the hospital's monitors provided a background hum as Erin sat at Emma's bedside, her hands clasped tightly in her lap. The muted light of the afternoon sun cast long shadows across the sterile white walls, making the room feel both too quiet and unbearably small. The scent of antiseptic lingered in the air, mixed with the faint aroma of the bouquet of sunflowers sitting by the window. Yet, even their cheerful presence couldn't dispel the weight of what needed to be said.

Erin had rehearsed this conversation over and over, yet now that the moment had come, her throat felt dry, her words stuck like unspoken grief in her chest.

Emma stirred slightly, turning her head toward Erin. Loose strands of hair framed her pale face, and though her body appeared frail, her eyes held the quiet strength that had always defined her.

"Mom?" Her voice was hoarse but steady. "What's wrong? You've been quiet all morning."

Erin's chest tightened. She took a deep breath and reached for her daughter's hand, feeling its fragile warmth beneath her fingers.

"Emma," she began softly, "there's something I need to tell you. I didn't want to say anything until you were strong enough."

Emma's expression shifted, concern knitting her brow. "What is it? Is Kate okay?"

"She's fine, sweetheart," Erin reassured her quickly. "She's recovering well. But this is about Mac."

The air seemed to thicken between them, and Emma's breath caught. "Mac?" Her voice was barely a whisper. "What about him?"

Erin hesitated, her own grief bubbling beneath the surface. "Mac... Mac didn't make it, honey. He was shot during the robbery." Her voice broke, and tears spilled down her cheeks. "He didn't survive."

Emma's face crumpled as the weight of the words sank in. She turned her head away, her breathing uneven. "No," she whispered, shaking her head. "Not Mac."

Erin leaned forward, her own tears falling freely. "I'm so sorry, Emma. I know how much he meant to you."

For several moments, neither of them spoke. Emma's shoulders trembled as silent sobs overtook her. "He was like a father to me," she said finally, her voice raw with pain. "He believed in me, Mom. He... he was always there."

Erin tightened her grip on Emma's hand. "I know, sweetheart. And he loved you like his own."

Emma closed her eyes, tears slipping down her cheeks. Memories of Mac's booming laughter, his steady presence, and the stories he would tell as she and her father, Ryan, sipped coffee at his shop swirled in her mind. "Why did this happen, Mom? Why him?"

Erin had no answers, only the aching truth that life was often cruel in ways that defied understanding. "I don't know, Emma," she said quietly. "But I do know he would want you to focus on healing. He would want you to live your life fully—just like he lived his."

***

That night, Emma tossed and turned in her hospital bed, sleep eluding her. When it finally came, it brought no solace.

In her dream, the scene at Mac's replayed with agonizing clarity. The deafening crack of gunfire. Mac's body crumpling to the ground. The searing pain as bullets tore into her side. She woke with a start, her heart pounding and her breaths ragged. The sterile hospital room around her was dimly lit, the blinking monitors offering the only illumination.

She pressed a hand to her bandaged side, tears streaming down her face. Gratitude for surviving mingled with the suffocating weight of guilt and grief. How could she feel thankful when Mac was gone?

***

The next afternoon, Dave arrived at the hospital, his presence a welcome distraction. He knocked lightly on the doorframe before stepping inside, the scent of his aftershave blending with the sterile hospital air. In his hands was a bouquet of cheerful sunflowers, their bright petals a stark contrast to his police dress uniform he still wore from earlier that morning.

"Hey, partner," he said, his voice warm but carrying a hint of exhaustion. "You're looking better."

Emma managed a weak smile as Dave replaced the flowers on the windowsill. But as she took in his somber expression and the way he carried himself, a realization dawned on her.

"You went to Mac's funeral," she said softly.

Dave nodded, his usual easy demeanor subdued. He pulled a chair to her bedside and sat down, his hands clasped together as he let out a slow breath. "Yeah. The whole department turned out. You should've seen it, Em. Officers from all over Raleigh showed up. Not just the guys from our precinct—everyone. Mac was one of us."

Emma swallowed hard, her throat thick with emotion. "I wish I could have been there."

"I know," Dave said gently. "I wish you could've been too. His family… they were given a posthumous award from the department for his years of support. You know how Mac was. That shop was more than just a business—it was a second home for half the officers in this city. He always had a fresh pot of coffee, a joke, and a story ready."

Emma's lips trembled as she nodded. "I can still hear his laugh. Smell that awful burnt coffee he refused to throw out."

Dave chuckled softly. "Yeah. And that ancient radio playing the same classic rock station for decades. I think half the officers in Raleigh had their first cup of coffee at Mac's."

Emma exhaled shakily, her fingers gripping the hospital blanket. "I don't know how to do this, Dave. How do I walk into that shop again? How do I accept that he's gone?"

Dave reached out, gently covering her hand with his own. His touch was steady, reassuring. "You don't have to figure that out today. You don't have to figure it out alone."

Emma looked at him then, really looked at him. There was something unspoken in the way he held her gaze, something deeper than friendship, something she hadn't quite been ready to acknowledge before. And now, in the quiet space between grief and healing, she felt the stirrings of something new—something terrifying but not unwelcome.

"Thank you," she whispered.

Dave's fingers tightened around hers for just a second before he let go, his smile soft. "Anytime, partner. Anytime."

And as he sat with her in the dim hospital room, Emma realized that maybe—just maybe—she wasn't as alone as she had thought.

Chapter 9

The Weight of Trauma

The morning sun peeked through the blinds of Emma's hospital room, but its warmth did little to ease the chill she felt inside. She sat up in her bed, her knees drawn to her chest, her head resting on her arms. Tears streamed silently down her face.

Restless nights had begun to take their toll—shadows clung beneath her eyes, and her thoughts felt scattered. Every time she closed her eyes, the scene replayed: the flash of a gun, Mac's body crumpling, and the sharp, searing pain as her own body hit the floor.

The nurses and doctors were kind, but their words of encouragement felt hollow. She couldn't shake the feeling that the world she had once known—her sense of safety and purpose—had shattered in those terrifying moments.

Dr. Calloway entered Emma's room, his warm smile tempered with concern. Erin, seated beside Emma, straightened as the doctor spoke.

"Emma, I've asked someone to meet with you today—a psychiatrist named Dr. Rachel Lawson. She's very experienced in helping people process trauma, and I think she can offer you some guidance as you navigate what you're feeling."

Emma nodded slowly, her voice subdued. "I think I'd like that. I don't want to feel like this forever."

Dr. Calloway placed a reassuring hand on her shoulder. "That's a good first step, Emma. You're already stronger than you realize."

Later that morning, Dr. Lawson arrived, her demeanor calm and approachable. She introduced herself to Emma and began the conversation gently.

"Emma, I know you've been through a lot. I want you to know that everything you're feeling—the grief, the fear, the exhaustion—it's normal after what you've experienced. You've been incredibly strong just to get to this point."

Emma hesitated before speaking. "I keep having nightmares… about the robbery, about Mac. I wake up, and it's like I'm right back there." Her voice trembled, and tears filled her eyes.

Dr. Lawson nodded. "Those are classic signs of post-traumatic stress disorder (PTSD). The good news is there are ways to work through it—tools to help you regain control. But it's a journey, Emma. One step at a time."

They spent the session exploring Emma's feelings and laying the groundwork for coping strategies. Dr. Lawson also assured her that therapy would be part of her recovery, both in and out of the hospital.

Later that afternoon, a light knock sounded on the door before Dave stepped inside. He carried his usual easy confidence, but there was a gentleness in his expression as he took in Emma's weary face.

"Hey, partner," he said, setting a small paper bag on the table beside her bed. "Thought you could use a decent cup of coffee. The hospital stuff is terrible."

Emma gave a faint smile as she took the cup, the warmth seeping into her hands. She breathed in deeply, letting the rich aroma cut through the hospital's sterile scent. "Thanks, Dave."

He pulled up a chair beside her, leaning in slightly. "How are you really doing?"

Emma hesitated before answering, her fingers tracing the rim of the coffee cup. "I just want to go home," she admitted, her voice quieter than usual.

Dave's brows furrowed. "Back to your place in Raleigh?"

She shook her head, her gaze drifting toward the window. "No... home home. Linville."

Dave nodded slowly, watching the way her face softened at the mention of the small mountain town. "I don't think I've ever heard you talk about Linville much. I knew Mac fished with you there."

Emma exhaled, as if summoning the right words. "It's where I grew up. My dad used to take me fly-fishing there, along the Linville River. Mac would join us sometimes. It was... our thing.

Just the rhythm of the water, the sound of the line whipping through the air, the quiet between casts." She paused, her voice thick with emotion. "It's the one place where everything makes sense. Where I feel connected—to my dad, to Mac, to the world."

Dave watched her carefully, absorbing the depth of what she was sharing. This wasn't just about fishing. This was about healing, about reaching for something steady in the storm of grief.

"I'd love to see it," he said quietly.

Emma blinked, caught off guard. "Really?"

He nodded. "Yeah. I've never been fly-fishing, but if it means that much to you... I'd like to learn."

Emma studied him for a moment, searching for any hint of obligation in his voice. But all she saw was sincerity. A warmth spread through her, something different than friendship, something deeper.

A slow smile touched her lips. "I think you'd like it," she said. "It's not just about catching fish. It's about patience, about being part of something bigger than yourself. Feeling the river move around you, the way everything slows down. It's... peaceful."

Dave held her gaze, and for the first time since she had woken up in the hospital, she felt understood in a way that had nothing to do with words. "Sounds like exactly what you need right now," he murmured.

She nodded, swallowing against the emotion tightening her throat. "Yeah. It is."

A comfortable silence stretched between them before Dave reached out, his fingers brushing over the back of her hand. It was a small gesture, but one that sent warmth up Emma's arm.

"You let me know when you're ready," he said. "I'll be there."

Emma's heart beat a little faster, not from fear or grief this time but from something new—something she wasn't sure she was ready to name just yet. But as she squeezed his hand in return, she knew one thing for certain.

She wasn't alone in this anymore.

The quiet hum of the hospital corridor was interrupted by a sharp knock on the door. Emma looked up to see Chief Williams step inside, his towering frame commanding the room.

"Chief," Emma said, surprised.

The older man smiled warmly, pulling up a chair next to Dave. "I wanted to see how you're doing, Emma. You've had the entire department worried."

"I'm healing," Emma replied, her tone formal but grateful.

Chief Williams leaned forward, his voice gentle. "Listen, Emma. You've been through something most people can't even imagine. I want you to take all the time you need to recover. Don't rush back to the force. The job will be there when you're ready."

Emma nodded, her eyes glistening. "Thank you, Chief. That means a lot."

The chief's gaze softened. "Your father would be proud of you, Emma. He always talked about how you had a fire in you—a determination to make the world better. Take care of yourself. That's how you honor him, too."

As Chief Williams left, Erin entered the room and sat down next to Dave in the chair by Emma's bedside. She reached out and gently stroked her daughter's face.

"You're so much like your dad," Erin said softly. "Strong, stubborn, and brave. But even he would tell you to take this one step at a time."

Emma smiled faintly, leaning into her mother's touch. "I'll try, Mom. I promise."

That evening, as Emma lay awake, her mind drifted to Linville, to the river, and to the promise of something more between her and Dave.

For the first time in a long while, hope didn't feel so far away.

Chapter 10

Hospital to Linville

As the days in the hospital stretched on, Emma found herself yearning for a change of scenery. The sterile white walls, the constant beeping of monitors, and the faint, metallic scent of antiseptic clung to her senses like an oppressive fog. Though her body was healing, the weight of Mac's death and the trauma she'd endured settled deep in her bones, a shadow that refused to lift.

On the morning of her discharge, Erin arrived early, her presence as warm and steady as ever. She smoothed a stray strand of hair from Emma's forehead, her touch gentle but firm. "Are you ready to come home?" she asked softly, her eyes searching Emma's face for any hesitation.

Emma exhaled slowly, her breath tinged with uncertainty but also relief. "Yeah. I think I need it."

The hospital staff completed the final paperwork, and within an hour, Emma was carefully settled into the passenger seat of Erin's SUV, the seat belt snug across her torso, pressing lightly against her still healing wounds. In her lap, she held the Statement of Fitness for Work note from Dr. Calloway—*Ms. Patterson may return to normal activities six weeks after surgery.* The words felt distant, almost impersonal, as if they failed to acknowledge the deeper scars left behind.

The drive from Raleigh to Linville stretched long and quiet, the hum of the tires on asphalt a steady backdrop to their thoughts. Outside, the world unfolded in a blur of shifting landscapes— flatlands gave way to rolling hills, which gradually climbed into the rugged majesty of the Blue Ridge Mountains. The air grew cooler, carrying the crisp scent of pine and damp earth, tinged with the lingering freshness of recent rain.

Erin stole a glance at Emma. "How are you feeling?"

Emma shifted slightly, wincing at the ache in her side. "Sore. Tired. But better now that we're almost there."

The road wound its way through dense forests, the trees stretching high overhead, their golden and russet leaves whispering in the wind. Emma cracked the window, inhaling deeply. The scent of home—mountain air, the faintest hint of woodsmoke—wrapped around her like an old friend.

When they finally pulled into Erin's driveway, Emma's breath hitched. The house stood just as she remembered—white shutters, a wraparound porch lined with rocking chairs, and a wind chime tinkling in the breeze. The sight tugged at something deep inside her, a nostalgia laced with both comfort and longing.

Erin parked and quickly moved to Emma's side, opening the door before she had the chance to struggle with it herself. "Easy, sweetheart," she murmured, offering her arm for support.

Emma let her mother help her inside, her steps slow but determined. The moment she crossed the threshold, the scent of cinnamon tea and aged oak filled her senses. A fire crackled in the hearth, casting flickering shadows against the warm, honey-toned walls. Daniel Campbell had used the spare key under the planter on the porch to let himself in to prepare the fire and make a pot of tea for Erin and Emma's return. It was a welcome surprise for both, thanks to Kate's gentle prodding of her dad to make for a nice homecoming.

"You'll have your old room," Erin said, leading her down the hall. "But if you'd rather something different, we can move things around."

Emma shook her head, exhaustion settling deep in her limbs. "No, this is perfect, Mom."

That night, she curled beneath a thick, handmade quilt, the weight of it grounding her. Outside, crickets chirped in rhythmic harmony, a lullaby only the mountains could provide. It wasn't an escape from her grief, but it was a step toward something resembling peace.

***

Back in Raleigh, the atmosphere in the precinct was a stark contrast to the quiet serenity of Linville. The conference room was dimly lit, illuminated only by the overhead projector casting a cold glow over the evidence board. Dave stood at the head of the table, his jaw tight, his eyes scanning the faces of his small but determined team of undercover officers. The recent string of fentanyl overdoses had led them to a network of distributors operating under the radar, and Mac's murder had only intensified their pursuit.

Detective Raines, a wiry man with sharp eyes and a perpetual five-o'clock shadow, tapped a pen against a photograph of a known distributor. "We've traced the supply chain back to two key players. One of them is tied to the same crew that hit the store."

Dave folded his arms across his chest, his muscles tense beneath his shirt. "Then we take them down." His voice was measured, but the fire in his eyes betrayed the storm raging inside him.

Chief Williams strode into the room, his presence commanding. He didn't waste time with pleasantries. "I know this case is personal for you," he said, his gaze locking onto Dave's. "But I need you to stay sharp. No reckless moves."

Dave met the chief's eyes, his voice steady but edged with resolve. "I understand, Chief. But I'm seeing this through."

Williams studied him for a long moment before nodding. "Good. Keep me updated."

Over the next few days, the task force moved like a well-oiled machine—stakeouts, coded exchanges, quiet negotiations with informants. Each thread they pulled unraveled more of the tangled web, bringing them closer to the core of the operation. But with each step forward came an increasing sense of danger.

Late one evening, Dave sat in his unmarked car outside a rundown apartment complex, watching a suspected dealer through a pair of binoculars. The night air was thick with the scent of damp pavement and lingering exhaust fumes. Inside the building, shadows shifted behind curtained windows, brief flickers of movement betraying unseen figures.

His phone buzzed. A message from Erin: *Emma's adjusting. She has good days and bad days, but being here is helping.*

Dave exhaled slowly, the tension in his shoulders easing just slightly. He imagined Emma back in Linville, the quiet strength in her eyes, the way she had always carried herself—resilient, determined, even in the face of overwhelming loss.

A voice crackled through his earpiece, snapping him back to the moment. "Target's on the move."

Dave straightened, his grip tightening on the steering wheel. Emma was healing, finding her way back to herself. And soon, justice for Mac—and for every life stolen by the poison infecting the streets—would follow.

He started the car, determination solidifying into something unshakable.

The hunt wasn't over. Not yet.

Chapter 11

Farmwork

It is said that you can see as far as an eagle from the right spot on Grandfather Mountain. The Cherokee once called it "Tanawha," meaning "great hawk"—a fitting name for a peak that has watched over the valleys for centuries. Even now, as Emma climbed, her breath coming in shallow gulps, she wondered how many generations had stood in this very spot, taking in the view that stretched for miles in every direction.

No matter how high I climb up this pile of dirt and stone, I feel like I can't see what is five feet in front of me.

She pushed herself harder, her boots crunching against loose rock as she ascended a steep incline. Her muscles burned, but she welcomed the sensation. With each step, the wind carried the crisp scent of spruce and damp earth, mingled with the faintest whisper of honeysuckle clinging stubbornly to the rocky ledges. It was a scent that had lived in her bones since childhood, woven into her memories of exploring these trails with her father and Mac.

At last, she reached a plateau where her 2016 Jeep Wrangler Sahara 4x4 was parked. Leaning against the tailgate, she wiped the sweat from her brow with a towel and took a long sip from a tepid bottle of water. The wind lifted strands of her hair, cooling the perspiration on her skin. Below her, the rolling valleys of Linville spread out like a quilt of emerald and gold, stitched together by winding streams and dense spruce-fir forests. The sight filled her with an aching nostalgia—this land had been her sanctuary long before the chaos of city life had stolen her away.

She exhaled deeply. "Back to work."

The drive down the mountain was as familiar as breathing. She navigated the narrow roads, passing beneath towering eastern hemlocks, red spruce, and Fraser firs that had stood guard for centuries. A sign for Linville flashed by, and she turned onto a dirt road nearly hidden by overgrown laurel. The tires of her Jeep jostled over the rocky remnants of an old riverbed before the path smoothed into a gentle incline. As she rounded the last bend, the sight of the homestead came into view—white clapboard walls, a sturdy wraparound porch, and the barn standing proud against the backdrop of the Blue Ridge Mountains.

Her great-great grandparents had built this place with their own hands, carving out a life in a land once home to the Cherokee before early settlers arrived. Scottish immigrants, drawn by the familiarity of the rugged terrain, they had made Linville their home in the late 1700s. They brought with them their traditions—Highland games, the mournful wail of bagpipes, and the art of storytelling passed from father to son. The very land seemed to hum with their legacy.

From the barn's shadow emerged Teddy, the aging blind gray mule, his long ears twitching at her arrival. His bray was a deep, rolling sound that echoed across the valley.

"That old mule is like a puppy around you, Emma," Erin called from the front porch, a metal bowl resting in her lap as she snapped green beans with practiced ease. The crisp snap echoed in the quiet air. "Come give me a hand and tell me about your day."

Emma stepped out of the Jeep, stretching her stiff limbs. "Mom, I don't have time. I need to milk the goats."

Erin smirked, tossing a bean pod into the bowl. "That's your way of saying you don't want to talk yet."

Emma offered an apologetic smile before striding toward the barn, Teddy plodding along beside her like a faithful companion.

Inside, the earthy scent of hay mixed with the musky aroma of the animals. Dust motes floated in the fading sunlight that streamed through the wooden slats. Lucy and Ethel, her Alpine goats, greeted her with expectant bleats, their eyes bright with mischief.

"All right, ladies, let's get this done."

She led Lucy onto the milking stand, securing her gently. With practiced hands, she cleaned the udder with warm water before positioning a stainless steel bucket beneath her. The rhythmic sound of milk streaming into the pail was oddly soothing, the familiar cadence grounding her in the present.

"Lucy, what do you have for me today? Let's see if you can fill this bucket."

Milk frothed as it pooled in the pail. Ethel, ever impatient, stomped a hoof, eager for her turn.

"Relax, girl," Emma murmured, chuckling as she finished with Lucy and moved to Ethel. "You'd think I was starving you."

Once the milking was complete, she strained the milk into mason jars, twisting on lids before tucking them into the old refrigerator in the corner of the barn. She leaned against the wooden counter, running a hand over Lucy's back as she listened to the quiet rustling of the animals settling in for the evening.

Outside, the sky had deepened to a warm amber, the scent of Erin's cooking drifting on the cooling breeze. Hints of rosemary and roasted chicken mingled with the lingering aroma of wood smoke curling from the chimney.

As Emma walked toward the house, she let her fingers trail over the weathered wood of the porch railing. For the first time in weeks, the ever-present weight pressing against her chest felt lighter. The mountain, the farm, the simple act of tending to the animals—it was all a part of her, stitched into her very being.

Tonight, she would sit at the worn oak table, share a meal with her mother, and listen to the crickets serenade the night. Tomorrow, the world and its battles would still be there, waiting.

But tonight she was home.

Chapter 12

A Gift from Raleigh

When Dave pulled up to the farm with the horse trailer, Emma's curiosity piqued. She stood on the porch, wiping her hands on her apron, the scent of freshly baked cornbread clinging to the fabric. The morning sun cast a golden hue over the rolling pastures, its warmth mixing with the crisp, scented air. She squinted as Dave stepped out of his truck, his boots crunching against the gravel driveway.

As the trailer creaked open, a small, shaggy Shetland pony stepped hesitantly onto the wooden ramp, blinking against the bright sunlight. Its mane was a tangled mess, a patchwork of white and chestnut-brown, and its short legs trembled slightly as it adjusted to the new surroundings. The sight was so unexpected, so utterly out of place, that Emma let out a surprised laugh.

Dave glanced at her, rubbing the back of his neck. "It's from Raleigh," he explained, his voice rough, betraying an emotion he wasn't quite ready to name. "The pony was abandoned at the police station. No one knew what to do with him, so I thought... maybe you could help." He hesitated, then took a step closer, lowering his voice. "I figured I couldn't give you Mac back, but maybe this would help. For what it's worth... I'm sorry, Emma."

The words carried on the wind, settling between them like the first leaves of autumn. Emma's throat tightened as she looked at him. The sorrow in his eyes was unspoken but palpable, like an echo of her own grief. She exhaled slowly, running her fingers through the pony's unruly mane.

"You're a fool," she murmured, her voice soft, tinged with amusement. "But I'll take him."

Dave nodded, relief flickering across his face. He led the pony toward the barn, its hooves clopping against the dirt path, and called over his shoulder, "I'll wait for you by the river."

The Linville River was a ribbon of silver in the afternoon light, its waters tumbling over smooth stones, whispering secrets to the ancient trees that lined its banks. Emma adjusted her fishing vest, the scent of damp earth and river moss filling her senses, and handed Dave a fly rod. He took it awkwardly, his fingers tightening around the cork handle like it might bite him.

"Alright, Dave. First things first—let me show you how to cast." She moved beside him, their shoulders almost brushing. "It's not like regular fishing. The line needs to be light and delicate."

Dave watched her intently as she demonstrated, the smooth motion of her wrist guiding the line in a fluid arc before it landed on the water's surface with barely a ripple. He tried to mimic her, but his first attempt sent the line flopping unceremoniously a few feet in front of them. Emma stifled a laugh.

"You've got the patience of a saint, you know that?" he muttered, adjusting his stance.

She smirked. "Patience is all part of it. You won't catch a thing if you rush."

For the next hour, Dave practiced, his movements becoming less rigid with each cast. The sun dipped lower, painting the sky in hues of amber and rose. The rhythmic sounds of the river, the chirping of distant cicadas, and the occasional splash of a fish breaking the surface created a symphony of stillness and life.

It was during one of these quiet moments that Dave spoke, his voice carrying just above the river's hum. "My heart's in the Highlands."

Emma looked up, surprised. "Burns?"

Dave shrugged, his expression almost sheepish. "Yeah. My mom used to make me recite it when I was a kid. I had a speech problem, you know. She said poetry would help me find my voice."

Emma tilted her head, watching him more closely. She had always known Dave carried more beneath the surface than he let on, but this—the poetry, the vulnerability—was something new. Something raw.

"Do you ever forget it?" she asked.

He shook his head, a small, almost imperceptible smile playing on his lips. "Not really. It kind of sticks with you after a while. I guess that's what poetry does."

Emma let the silence settle, the weight of his words sinking in. She suddenly wanted to hear more—not just the poem, but the parts of Dave he rarely shared.

"Try it again," she encouraged.

Dave hesitated, then waded a little deeper into the river, the cool water swirling around his calves. His voice came steadier this time, the cadence smoothing out. "My heart's in the Highlands, my heart is not here." The words seemed to drift into the breeze, carried away like leaves on the current.

And then, as if the river had been listening, Dave's fly rod jerked in his hands. His eyes widened, and for a moment, he froze. Then, with a burst of excitement, he reeled in his line, a small trout wriggling at the end of the hook.

Emma laughed, the sound bright and unburdened. "See? You got it. Not bad for your first try."

Dave held up the fish, his face a mix of pride and disbelief. "I can't believe it. I actually did it." He turned to her, his eyes shining with something lighter than she had seen in a long time. "Guess I'm not such a bad student after all."

Emma smiled, shaking her head. It wasn't just the fishing he was learning—it was how to trust, how to let go, and how to be patient with himself. And for the first time in a long while, Emma realized that maybe—just maybe—she was learning a little bit of the same thing.

Chapter 13

The Wooden Mountain

Lucy and Ethel were in full mischief mode, and Emma couldn't help but laugh as she watched them race around the backyard, their little hooves clattering against the ground. The Alpine goats were a handful, always into something. But today, they had found a new game—climbing the wooden crib next to the farmhouse. Emma's heart skipped a beat as the two goats scrambled up the stacked logs like mountain climbers, their eyes wide with excitement.

"Lucy! Ethel!" Emma called, though she knew they weren't about to listen. The goats had no concept of danger, and Emma's roof—well, it wasn't built to support their shenanigans.

She sighed, wiping her hands on her apron. "Every time, it's the roof."

From the kitchen window, Emma watched as Lucy made a daring leap from the top of the wooden crib onto the roof of the small room off the back of the house. Ethel followed with a bleat of triumph. The shingles, loosened by their weight, slid slightly out of place.

Emma didn't have time to stew in frustration. She grabbed the ladder from beside the barn and set it up, the familiar creak of wood under her hands comforting in its simplicity. As she climbed, she could hear the faint bleating of Lucy and Ethel as they proudly paraded across the roof. It was as if they knew they'd won some small victory.

"Alright, alright," Emma muttered to herself, hammer in hand. "One more thing to fix."

By the time she had nailed the shingles back into place, the goats had already moved on to their next adventure—eating her flower beds, no doubt.

As she stood on the ladder, gazing at the goats below, she heard the familiar rumble of a truck engine approaching. She glanced up just as Dave pulled into the driveway. His truck rolled to a stop with an almost comic slowness, and he got out, scratching his head at the sight before him.

"Are you... fixing your roof?" he asked, his voice a mix of confusion and amusement.

Emma chuckled and climbed down the ladder, brushing the dust from her hands. "The goats decided to redecorate."

Dave's eyes moved from the roof to the two goats, who were now bleating happily, as if celebrating their success. "I take it this isn't the first time?"

"Hardly," Emma replied with a knowing smile. "They've got a thing for heights."

Dave shook his head, clearly astonished. "I can't believe it. They actually climbed up there?"

"Yup. And now I get to be the one who fixes it."

There was a beat of silence before Dave offered a small, sheepish grin. "Well, I'm not the roof-fixing type, but... maybe I can help in another way."

Emma raised an eyebrow. "How's that?"

Dave gave a little shrug, as if the idea had just come to him. "I'll build them a mountain."

Emma blinked, not sure she'd heard him correctly. "A mountain?"

"You know, a wooden one. So they've got somewhere to climb that won't ruin your roof." Dave rubbed his hands together as if already picturing the project in his mind. "They seem like the type that need something to play on. I'll make it sturdy enough so they can't break it."

Emma's lips twitched, holding back a laugh. She had to admit the idea sounded as ridiculous as it was sweet. But there was something about Dave's earnestness that made it impossible to say no.

"Alright, Dave," she said, crossing her arms. "But no more climbing on my roof."

"I'll make sure of it," he replied, already headed to the barn, his voice carrying back to her. "I'll get to work. Meet you by the river later?"

Emma watched him go, her heart a little lighter than it had been a few minutes ago. There was something about the way Dave always showed up when she least expected it—how he had a way of making her feel like maybe, just maybe, life could be a little simpler again.

A couple of hours later, Dave stood proudly in front of the wooden structure he'd built. It wasn't exactly a mountain, but it was close enough—three tiers of wooden platforms, stacked high enough to keep the goats occupied without risking Emma's roof.

"Here it is," Dave said with a grin, wiping his hands on his jeans as he stepped back to admire his work. "It's not exactly the Alps, but it should keep them entertained."

Emma surveyed the wooden mountain, trying not to laugh at the sight. It was sturdy, practical, and had a certain charm to it. If anything, it was a testament to Dave's thoughtfulness, even if it did look a little out of place in the middle of her backyard.

"I can't believe you did this," she said, her voice a mix of amusement and gratitude.

Dave shrugged, still watching the goats inspect their new playground. "You should see the stuff I've built over the years. This one's nothing."

Emma smiled, touched by the effort he'd put in. It wasn't just about the goats. It was about him being here, showing up in ways she never expected but always needed.

She surveyed the mountain and gave it a name, testing the sound of it. "You know what? I think we'll call it the Brig o' Doon."

Dave looked over at her, brow furrowed in curiosity. "The Brig o' Doon?"

She grinned, knowing the moment was right. "It's from Robert Burns, Tam o' Shanter."

Dave's eyes lit up. "I didn't know you were into Burns." *Did Emma hear me recite Burns in the recovery room? Does she know how I feel about her?*

Emma shrugged, her tone playful. "I know a bit. That poem's always stuck with me. The Brig o' Doon was a metaphor for crossing over, leaving behind one part of life to enter another."

"Sounds fitting," Dave agreed. "A bridge. A place to cross into something new. But the full poem? Emma, that's one of the longest ones. You really want to hear it?"

She leaned against the fence, her expression curious but sincere. "You're right. It's a long one, but I think I'd like to hear it. But maybe not here... Not when there are goats to be entertained. Actually, Daniel Campbell, owner of The Stag & Thistle, is known to recite it on Halloween for a pint or two."

Dave chuckled. "Fair enough. I'd say it's worth at least a pint at The Stag & Thistle, and I would enjoy hearing Daniel."

Emma smiled, her gaze softening with a warmth she hadn't felt in a long while. Impulsively, she leaned in and pressed a gentle kiss to Dave's cheek. His skin was warm beneath her lips, and she could feel the brief hitch in his breath before he exhaled, steadying himself.

"You've got yourself a deal," she murmured, stepping back with a quiet smile.

Dave swallowed, a small, almost bashful grin tugging at the corners of his mouth. "Yeah... a deal."

As they both turned to watch the goats begin their first play on the wooden platform, Emma whispered under her breath, "The Brig o' Doon. A place to cross over... into something new."

Dave glanced over at her, catching the wistful smile on her lips. "I think you might be right, Emma. I think you might be right."

Chapter 14

The Stag & Thistle

The Raleigh Fentanyl Drug Task Force worked relentlessly, their war room humming with the low murmur of conversations, the rustle of case files, and the occasional sharp click of a marker against the evidence board. The fluorescent lights buzzed overhead, casting a sterile glow over the room's chaos—maps dotted with pushpins, surveillance photos taped in overlapping layers, and whiteboards filled with hastily scrawled notes and timelines.

Dave sat hunched over the main table, his fingers absently tapping a pen against the corner of a file. The stale scent of burnt coffee lingered in the air, mixing with the faint musk of paperwork and sweat from long hours of investigation. Across from him, Detective Raines flipped through reports, his brow furrowed in concentration.

Dave's gaze landed on a timeline chart pinned to the board. His mind worked through the pattern forming in front of him, puzzle pieces snapping into place. "Look at this," he muttered, tapping the board with the capped end of his pen. "The shipments are coming in every Tuesday—and distribution happens Wednesday. Always from that warehouse we've had under surveillance."

Raines leaned in, eyes narrowing as he traced the movements with his finger. "You're right," he said, voice low and measured. "That's our window. We'll set up the raid for Wednesday—catch them as soon as the next shipment hits." He exhaled sharply, already forming the next steps in his mind. The air in the room felt heavier, charged with the anticipation of a breakthrough.

***

Meanwhile, in Linville, Emma sat at the kitchen table, *The Avery Journal Times* spread open in front of her. The morning sunlight slanted through the window, casting golden patches on the wooden floor. The rich aroma of freshly brewed tea curled around her, blending with the faint scent of her mother's lavender-scented hand lotion.

Her eyes lingered on a job posting for a part-time opening at the local 911 center. The crisp paper crackled softly as she tapped a thoughtful finger against the ad. Maybe this is my way back in— a chance to help again, even in a small way.

"Mom?" Emma asked, glancing up. "What would you think if I applied for a part-time job at the 911 center?"

Erin looked up from her cup, the steam curling in delicate wisps around her face. A warm smile spread across her lips, eyes twinkling with encouragement. "Emma, that sounds perfect for you. You've always had a heart for helping people—and it'll get you out of the house."

Emma smiled back, a flicker of excitement sparking in her chest. "Thanks, Mom. I'll apply today—it's all online."

After breakfast, she helped clean up the kitchen before heading outside. The crisp autumn air greeted her, carrying the earthy scent of damp leaves and fresh hay. Teddy, her loyal blind mule, ambled close behind as she made her way to the barn. His fur smelled of warm straw, and when she reached out, his ears flicked at her touch, soft and velvety against her palm.

She moved through her morning chores—the rhythmic scattering of feed, the gentle clatter of eggs settling into a basket, the steady swish of milk streaming into a pail. Once the jars of fresh milk were sealed and packed, she loaded them into her truck, the scent of wood and leather filling the cab as she headed toward The Stag & Thistle.

***

The scent of sizzling bacon and fresh bread enveloped Emma as she stepped inside The Stag & Thistle. The low hum of morning chatter mingled with the occasional clink of coffee cups against saucers.

"Good morning, Emma!" Daniel's voice boomed from behind the grill, his accent thick with cheer. "Go ahead and put the bottles in the fridge. I'm planning a Cornish fish pie for dinner tonight. Check out the butter and cheese I made from the last batch!"

Emma peeked into the fridge, her eyes lighting up at the creamy butter and wedges of cheese, their golden surfaces smooth and rich. "Looks delicious," she said, grinning. "Hey, Daniel—when are you going to make ice cream?"

"Saturday, Em! You want to come down and help me?" Daniel teased, flipping a pancake with a practiced flick of the wrist.

"Sure—count me in," Emma replied, laughing. "Maybe I can convince Mom to come down tonight for that fish pie."

"That'd be wonderful. I'd love to have you both here for dinner," Daniel said warmly.

"It's a date," Emma called over her shoulder as she headed for the door.

***

Once home, Emma excitedly shared with Erin the details of the Cornish fish pie Daniel was making. Erin hesitated, wrapping her fingers around her mug, the ceramic warm against her skin. Since Ryan's death, she had avoided going out at night, reluctant to return to an empty, dark home.

Emma, anticipating her resistance, quickly added, "Daniel especially asked if you'd come."

Erin sighed, searching for an excuse, but Emma wasn't having it. With a teasing smile, she asked, "What are you afraid of? A little fun?"

Reluctantly, Erin gave in. "Fine. But if it's terrible, you owe me."

Emma grinned in triumph before stepping outside. The day hummed along as she worked, the scent of damp earth rising as she raked leaves, the crisp rustle filling the air. But after a while, she noticed something unusual—Teddy wasn't trailing at her heels like he normally did.

Her pulse quickened as she scanned the property. A flicker of gray in the distance caught her eye—Teddy, down in a ditch, motionless.

"Teddy!" she called, stepping closer. "Come on, boy. Let's go!"

But Teddy didn't move. His ears flicked in response, but his hooves remained planted.

Determined, Emma hurried to the barn, grabbed a moving strap, and looped it around his body. She pulled with all her strength, her boots digging into the soft earth, her muscles straining—but Teddy refused to budge.

Just then, Erin appeared, carrying a basket of freshly pulled carrots, their leafy green tops spilling over the edges. The earthy scent drifted through the air, and as soon as it reached Teddy's nose, his nostrils twitched, his lips quivered—and then, with surprising urgency, he lunged forward, following the scent. Erin took a slow step back, then another, leading Teddy right out of the ditch as he eagerly trailed behind her.

With a chuckle, Erin stroked Teddy's head and said, "He may not be able to see, but his nose still works just fine." Then, turning to Emma, she added with a knowing smile, "You just needed to find something he wanted more than staying stuck."

Emma watched them, Erin leading Teddy effortlessly where sheer force had failed, and thought to herself, *Now, isn't that true on so many levels?*

Chapter 15

Decisions Made

That evening at The Stag & Thistle, the pub pulsed with life. Low conversation hummed against the backdrop of clinking glasses, the occasional burst of laughter rippling through the warm air. Candlelight flickered across the polished wood, reflecting off the glass bottles lining the bar, casting amber shadows against the stone walls. The scent of baking crust and slow-simmered seafood enveloped the room, rich and comforting, wrapping around Emma and Erin as they settled at their usual corner table.

Daniel emerged from the kitchen, a steaming plate in each hand. The golden, buttered crust of the Cornish fish pie crackled under his knife as he portioned out generous servings. Beneath the surface, the creamy mash melded into the fragrant filling—a delicate balance of flaky white fish, smoked haddock, and tender shrimp, all swimming in a silken béchamel laced with fresh herbs.

Erin took her first bite, her fork sliding through the layers effortlessly. The moment the flavors hit her tongue, she closed her eyes, exhaling softly. "Oh, Daniel, this is incredible."

Daniel's lips curled into a slow, pleased grin, his gaze lingering on the way Erin savored each bite. "Glad you approve," he murmured, feigning casualness, though he took careful note of every flicker of pleasure on her face.

The conversation meandered like the gentle stream outside the pub—drifting through talk of the recent storms, the upcoming county fair, and the latest town gossip. But when Daniel mentioned property tax bills, Emma noticed the subtle shift in Erin's demeanor. Her mother's shoulders stiffened almost imperceptibly.

"Has it gone up much this year?" Erin asked, her voice controlled, though her fingers absently pushed a single pea across her plate.

Daniel leaned back with a heavy sigh. "Yeah. Hit my homestead and the pub. It's steep this time around."

Emma didn't miss the flicker of unease in Erin's eyes. The numbers were tight—she knew that. The farm, once manageable under Ryan's care, now bore an invisible weight on Erin's shoulders. Emma swallowed down a sip of cider, letting the crisp apple and hint of spice linger on her tongue before setting the glass down with quiet resolve.

She had made her decision. She would apply for the 911 operator job. Her mother had sacrificed enough. Emma would do her part.

***

Across the state, in the cold embrace of an industrial district in Raleigh, the air carried a different kind of weight.

Dave sat with Detective Raines in an unmarked car, the leather seat beneath him creaking as he shifted his grip on the radio. Outside, the dim glow of sodium streetlights stretched long shadows across the pavement. The warehouse ahead, an unassuming hulk of concrete and steel, held the promise of a long-awaited break in the case.

At precisely 7:03 a.m., headlights cut through the thinning mist as a black Suburban rolled up to the loading dock. The driver idled for a beat before stepping out, his breath curling in the cool morning air. He scanned his surroundings, then disappeared through the entrance.

Minutes ticked by. Then the garage door groaned open, and the SUV eased inside.

Raines didn't hesitate. "Go."

Boots hit the pavement. Shadows surged forward. Weapons were drawn, muzzles steady in the dim light. With one fluid motion, the task force breached the building.

Chaos erupted.

"Down on the ground! Now!"

Shouts ricocheted off the warehouse walls. A man bolted toward the exit—Dave lunged, tackling him to the concrete. A struggle ensued, limbs tangling, the sharp sting of asphalt burning through Dave's sleeve as they hit the ground. A sharp elbow to his ribs sent a jolt of pain up his side, but he countered with a swift twist, pinning the suspect beneath him.

"Don't move," Dave growled, snapping the cuffs around the man's wrists.

The room reeked of chemical bitterness—fentanyl dust clung to every surface. Plastic bags, digital scales, and mixing trays littered the metal tables. And then there were the stacks of bricks. Over 200 pounds of pure poison.

Dave exhaled sharply. They had just prevented thousands of deaths. Maybe more.

But as officers secured the scene, his mind drifted elsewhere.

Emma.

He leaned against a desk, staring at his phone, his fingers twitching against the plastic casing. The weight of the case had consumed his days and nights, but she had never left his thoughts. The moment his head hit the pillow, the echo of her laughter filled the silence. The way she looked when she wasn't aware anyone was watching—soft, thoughtful, strong.

When would he finally get to tell her everything?

Because tonight, after months of chasing shadows, he wanted nothing more than to hear her voice.

Chapter 16

The Bigger Picture

Emma stands at the kitchen sink, rinsing the last of the breakfast dishes, when she hears it—the deep, familiar rumble of a truck making its way up the long gravel drive. She stills, her hands resting in the warm water, her heart giving a quiet stutter.

It's Dave.

He steps out of the truck just as she moves to the porch. He looks different—maybe it's the weight lifted from his shoulders after the long months of secrecy, or maybe it's the exhaustion still clinging to him from the job. Either way, he's here now, and Emma isn't sure how she feels about it.

For months, he had kept the truth from her—his undercover work with the drug task force, the danger he'd willingly thrown himself into while she was left in the dark. She doesn't know whether to be angry or relieved.

Dave watches her carefully as he approaches, measuring her expression. How will she take it? He hopes she understands why he couldn't tell her. That she'll see the bigger picture—that lives were saved, the streets were safer. That keeping her in the dark wasn't about deception, but about protection.

"I took a few days off," he says finally, stopping a few steps from her. "Wanted to see you."

Emma crosses her arms, leaning against the porch railing. "And tell me the whole truth this time?"

The corner of his mouth tugs upward—only slightly. He deserves that.

"Yeah," he says, his voice softer now. "That's the plan."

She doesn't say anything right away, just studies him the way she does when she's sorting through her thoughts. But then, just as she's about to speak, Dave lifts something from the bed of his truck—a brand-new fly rod and a small tackle box.

Emma raises an eyebrow. "Since when do you fish?"

"Since I figured out it might be the only way to get some uninterrupted time with you." He smirks. "And I hear the Linville's got some decent trout."

Emma can't help it—she laughs. It's short, unexpected, but real.

"Dave—" she starts, but then stops, shifting on her feet. There's something she needs to tell him, and she doesn't want to dance around it. "I'm going back to work."

He blinks. "Work?"

"I got a job. As a 911 operator."

Dave's easy demeanor shifts. His jaw tightens, just a fraction, but enough for her to notice.

Emma doesn't have to guess what he's thinking. Erin must have told him about the night terrors. About the way she still wakes up gasping, haunted by the shooting at Mac's.

"Are you sure that's what you want?" he asks carefully.

"I need to do something," she says, lifting her chin. "I need to help. And I can handle it."

Dave exhales through his nose, nodding slowly. He doesn't want to doubt her. He knows she's strong, but he also knows that strength doesn't mean unbreakable.

He lets it go—for now.

Later, at the river, they stand knee-deep in the cool water, casting their lines in silence. Hours pass this way—no words, just the rhythmic whisper of rods slicing through the air, the bubbling song of the current, and the occasional glance exchanged between them.

There's something healing in it, this quiet companionship. The unspoken understanding.

Then Dave spots it—a wild rose blooming on the far bank, delicate and defiant against the wilderness around it. Without thinking, he speaks, his voice low and steady over the water:

"O my Love is like a red, red rose

That's newly sprung in June;

O my Love is like the melody

That's sweetly played in tune."

Emma turns to him, a slow, knowing smile playing on her lips.

"You find poetry in everything," she says.

"Maybe," he replies, reeling in his line. "Or maybe I just see the poetry around me."

She studies him, her smile fading into something softer, something deeper.

Dave steps closer, his boots sinking into the wet sand as he reaches for her, hesitant at first, as if giving her space to pull away. But she doesn't. Instead, she tilts her face up toward his, her pulse thrumming in her throat.

And then, suddenly, the space between them disappears.

His lips meet hers in a slow, searching kiss, the kind that carries weight—the kind that says everything words can't. Emma's breath catches as warmth blooms in her chest, her hands sliding up to rest against his shoulders. He tastes of coffee and something unspoken, something that has always been between them but never acknowledged until now.

When they part, Dave's forehead rests lightly against hers. His voice is barely above a whisper, rough with emotion. "Emma, I'm in love with you."

Her heart stumbles, then soars. For so long, she had been afraid to name what had been growing between them, afraid to hope for something more. But standing here, with the river murmuring beside them and the golden light of dusk settling over the valley, she knows.

She loves him, too.

A smile spreads across her lips, slow and certain. "I think I've been waiting a long time to hear that."

He exhales a quiet chuckle, brushing a strand of hair from her cheek. "Yeah?"

"Yeah," she whispers, pressing another kiss to his lips. This time, there's no hesitation. No uncertainty. Just warmth, and belonging, and the quiet realization that, for the first time in a very long time—

She is happy.

Chapter 17

911, How Can I Help You?

E mma's first day at the 911 call center is a blur of voices, ringing phones, and the steady hum of controlled urgency. The fluorescent lights cast a stark glow over the room, the air thick with the scent of stale coffee and the faint tang of sweat. The training program has been intense—a week in the classroom followed by days of shadowing experienced operators, absorbing their calm under pressure like a lifeline. But now she's on her own. The headset rests snugly over her ears, her fingers poised over the keyboard, ready to answer the call that might mean the difference between life and death.

The calls vary—medical emergencies, domestic disputes, reports of prowlers in the dead of night. Some are frantic, others eerily calm, and each one requires quick thinking, steady hands, and a voice that doesn't waver. But nothing prepares her for the night that will shake her to her core.

The call comes in just after midnight. The voice on the other end is young and trembling.

"H-hello? Please, I need help."

Emma straightens, her pulse quickening. "This is 911. What's your emergency?"

"I... " The girl falters, her breath ragged, uneven. "I don't know where I am. He said he'd take me to town, but—he lied. He brought me to his house instead. I think it's in the woods. I don't know. I-I don't know what to do."

A chill runs down Emma's spine. The air in the call center suddenly feels too thick, the distant hum of other operators fading into the background. She focuses on the girl's voice, steadying her own.

"Are you safe right now?"

"I... I don't think so. He went outside, but he could come back any second."

Emma's fingers fly across the keyboard, flagging the call as high priority, her breath shallow as she alerts dispatch. The sound of keys clicking around her and the occasional murmur of other operators handling their own emergencies feels distant, secondary to the girl's uneven breaths in her ear.

"Okay, listen to me. Do you see any windows? Any landmarks?"

The girl sobs, her voice barely a whisper. "It's dark. There's... trees. A gravel road, I think."

Not enough. Not nearly enough.

"What's your name?"

"Kayla."

"Kayla, do you have an iPhone?

Kayla responds with "Yes."

Emma says, "Go to the home screen and let me know if you see a map. Tell me if it shows what road you're on."

Kayla fumbles, sniffles. "No map, it just says No Service. But I was able to call you."

Emma turns toward the dispatcher, her eyes urgent. "We need a trace."

The officer at the desk nods, fingers already flying over his own keyboard. "Triangulating," he confirms, but it takes time. Too much time.

Emma's voice is a lifeline, and she knows it. She takes a slow breath, steadying herself, forcing warmth into her tone despite the ice in her veins.

"Kayla, I need you to stay with me, okay? Focus on my voice."

A shaky inhale from the other end. "Okay."

"You're doing great. I promise I'm going to stay on the line with you. We're going to figure this out together."

A small whimper. "Okay."

Emma keeps her voice low and soothing, as if she and Kayla are sharing a secret. "Tell me everything you remember about how you got there. Did you drive long? Did you take turns?"

A sniffle. "Um... he drove. We were on a road with no streetlights. Just trees. A lot of trees. I thought we were going to town, but he never turned. Just kept driving."

Emma types rapidly, logging every detail. "Did you see any signs? Gas stations? Stores?"

Kayla is silent for a beat, then whispers, "There was a gas station before we turned onto the road. I think it had a blue sign."

Emma's pulse jumps. That's something. She turns to dispatch. "Find gas stations near the radius with blue signage."

She hears the tap of keys behind her as officers get to work. But they need more.

"Kayla, let's see if we can find something inside the house that tells us where you are. Can you describe the room you're in?"

Kayla takes a shuddering breath. "It smells... musty. Like... old wood? And something... weird. Like metal?"

Emma grips the edge of her desk. "Metal? Like pennies, like rust, or something else?"

"Rust. And something rotten. I don't know."

Emma's stomach turns. Blood? Decomposition? They need to move faster.

"Kayla, I know you're scared, but I need you to look around. Are there any papers? Magazines? Maybe an envelope?"

Rustling on the other end. A long pause. Then—

"There's... a piece of mail on the table. I can barely see it."

Emma leans forward, her heartbeat hammering. "Can you get closer? Can you read anything?"

A shuffle, a breath. Then Kayla's voice, barely above a whisper. "It says... Hollow Creek."

Emma whips around to dispatch. "Search for Hollow Creek in the radius!"

A nod from an officer. More typing. A response: "Got it! Hollow Creek Road—three properties in that area."

Emma's focus snaps back to Kayla. "You're doing so well. You're so strong. One last thing, okay? I need you to listen. Do you hear anything outside? Any cars, water, animals?"

Kayla holds her breath. Silence. Then—

"A creek. I think I hear water running somewhere."

That seals it. Emma relays the information. The officers have a target now.

A minute later, the radios crackle: "We've got a location. Suspect's inside. He's refusing entry."

Emma grips the edge of the desk, her knuckles white. The officers' voices on the radio are calm, but she can hear the tension beneath their words.

Sheriff Dobbs steps up to the front door, his voice even but firm. "Sir, we need to speak with the girl."

"She's fine," the man growls from inside. "She wants to be here."

The Sheriff doesn't buy it. "Then let us hear it from her."

Emma closes her eyes briefly. They found her.

"Kayla, help is there. I need you to stay calm. You're so close to being safe."

Kayla's breath hitches. "I hear them."

The back door bursts open, the sound of wood splintering sharp through the radio. Shouts, the scuffle of boots. The man struggles, cursing, but he's outnumbered. The metallic click of handcuffs snaps through the air like finality.

Kayla stumbles forward, into the waiting arms of a female officer.

Then the words Emma has been waiting for come across the radio: "Suspect in custody. Victim safe."

Emma exhales, her whole body sagging. Kayla sobs on the line, this time with relief.

"You did it," Emma whispers. "You got out."

Tears choke Kayla's response. "Thank you."

Emma pulls off her headset, rubbing her temples, her skin slick with a fine sheen of sweat. Relief washes over her, but so does something else—a familiar ache in her chest. The rush of adrenaline, the high of being in the moment… only this time, she wasn't out there. She was here. At a desk.

The coffee in her cup has gone cold, the fluorescent lights buzz softly overhead, and the stale air presses down on her like a heavy blanket.

The job is different, but the stakes are just as high. And tonight, she made a difference.

Maybe that's enough.

For now.

Chapter 18

A Sharp Crack

The house is still and quiet when Emma pulls into the driveway just before dawn. The sky is a bruised shade of blue, the last remnants of night clinging stubbornly to the horizon. A faint mist hovers over the ground, curling around the base of the porch like ghostly fingers. She steps out of the car, stretching, rolling her shoulders to shake off the stiffness from the long shift. The adrenaline from the night's call still hums in her veins, a restless energy refusing to settle.

Inside, the familiar scent of coffee lingers in the air, mingling with the faint aroma of cinnamon and toasted bread. The warmth of the house contrasts with the crisp morning air outside, and Emma exhales slowly, savoring the temporary cocoon of comfort. She presses her fingers against the still-warm coffee pot. Mom must be up.

She toes off her boots, careful to keep her steps light as she pads up the wooden stairs. The floorboards whisper beneath her weight, and she instinctively skips the creaky step near the top. As she reaches the landing, her mother's voice drifts from the bedroom, quiet but firm.

"And forgive us our trespasses, as we forgive those who trespass against us."

Emma freezes, her hand tightening around the banister. Forgiveness. The word slithers through her like a cold wind. How does someone forgive the unforgivable? How could Kayla ever forgive the man who stole her sense of safety? How could she forgive the men who killed Mac?

The thought knots inside her, heavy and sharp, but she forces it down. She moves forward, shutting her bedroom door behind her, blocking out the weight of the words.

***

Sleep is fitful. Dreams slip through her grasp like water, disjointed flashes of voices, of hands reaching, of the deep, hollow ring of silence. Five hours later, at 10 a.m., Emma wakes with a start, her body jerking upright, her breath ragged. Sunlight filters through the curtains in thin golden slats, dust particles swirling in the stillness.

The house is quiet, save for the faint hum of the wind through the trees. The stillness presses against her, too heavy, too loud in its own way. She needs to move. To breathe. To feel something other than this gnawing unease.

She dresses quickly, pulling on her boots and heading outside. The moment she steps onto the back porch, the scent of damp earth and pine fills her lungs, grounding her. The air is sharp and fresh, a contrast to the lingering staleness of the call center.

The farm is as it always is—steady, unwavering. The chickens rustle in their coop, their soft clucks breaking the quiet morning. The horses in the paddock flick their tails lazily, their breath visible in the cool air. And Teddy, ever her shadow, watches her with those intelligent eyes, his body tense with silent anticipation.

Still, the unease lingers.

"Forgiveness," she mutters under her breath, kicking at a loose stone on the path. The word tastes bitter. Is it even possible?

Fishing. Maybe that will clear her head. It always has.

She gathers her gear with familiar ease, the motions comforting. Teddy bounds alongside her as they head toward the river, his short, fine gray hair catching the morning light. The Linville River is a steady companion, its waters whispering against the rocks, the air cool and rich with the scent of moss and wet stone.

At the bank, Emma kneels, flipping over stones, studying the insects clinging beneath them. Her father had taught her this— always know what's happening under the surface. The memory softens something inside her, warming the raw edges of her mind.

She selects the right nymph, ties it onto her line, then wades into the water. The river nudges against her legs, cool and insistent. The rhythm of casting takes over, muscle memory guiding her as she flicks the line six feet upstream, letting it drift naturally.

A tug.

She sets the hook, her rod bending as the trout fights back. A sharp thrill shoots through her veins, momentarily pushing everything else aside. After a brief struggle, she reels it in—a beautiful ten-inch trout, its silver scales glinting like liquid metal.

Carefully, she removes the hook, her fingers deft despite the tremble beneath her skin. Lowering the fish back into the water, she watches it vanish into the current.

"Today's your day," she murmurs.

She shifts her stance, preparing for another cast, but her boot slides over something slick—a moss-covered rock. Her breath catches as her arms pinwheel, searching for balance.

Then the world tilts.

Cold.

A shocking, biting cold that clamps down on her lungs like a vise. The river swallows her, dragging her beneath its surface. Her boots, waterlogged and heavy, pull her down.

A sharp crack. Pain explodes at the back of her skull. A burst of white—then darkness.

The river moves on, indifferent.

Teddy's sharp, high-pitched whine cuts through the morning stillness. He circles the edge of the water, his tail low, his ears flattened against his head. He gives out a high-pitched squeal signaling distress—frantic, desperate. The fishing rod drifts downstream, swallowed by the current.

***

Back at the house, Erin hums softly as she folds linens, careful not to disturb the fragile morning peace. She knows Emma worked the night shift and doesn't want to wake her too soon. Still, a mother's instinct is hard to ignore.

As she moves down the hall, she pauses at Emma's room. The door is ajar. The bed unmade.

Frowning, she glances toward the window. Emma's car is still in the driveway.

A flicker of unease tightens in her chest.

Setting the linens aside, she heads outside, scanning the usual places.

No sign of her in the barn.

The paddock? Empty, save for the grazing horses.

Then she notices it—Teddy is gone, too.

Her heartbeat quickens.

She grabs the keys to the side-by-side, her pulse pounding as she drives toward the river. The deeper she goes into the woods, the more the unease grows, curling around her ribs like ice.

Then she sees him.

Teddy.

Standing on the shore, unmoving, his body rigid, his ears locked toward the water.

Something is wrong.

Erin's breath catches. She slams the brakes, the vehicle skidding to a stop. Her stomach drops as she follows Teddy's gaze.

There, half-submerged in the shallows, is Emma.

"Oh my God."

Erin is out of the vehicle in seconds, running, splashing into the water. The cold bites at her legs, but she barely notices.

Emma is pale, her lips slightly parted. Unmoving.

"Come on, baby, stay with me," Erin pleads, her voice raw as she grips Emma beneath her arms, dragging her onto the shore. The weight of her daughter's soaked body is a cruel reality in her hands.

With trembling fingers, she fumbles for her phone, dialing with frantic urgency.

"911, what's your emergency?"

Erin barely hears the dispatcher over the roar of her own pulse. "My daughter—she's unconscious by the Linville River. She's not waking up."

She presses her hand against Emma's cheek, willing her to open her eyes.

Teddy whines, nudging Emma's limp hand, his tail tucked tight against his body.

The wind whispers through the trees. The river flows on, indifferent.

For Erin, everything else has stopped.

"Hold on, sweetheart," she whispers. "Help is coming."

Chapter 19

Back to Hospital

The call went out across the Linville-Central Rescue Squad's radio just before 11:15 a.m.

"Female, unconscious, found near the Linville River. Possible head injury. Caller reports patient is breathing but unresponsive."

Within minutes, sirens pierced the morning air as the rescue squad's ambulance and a support vehicle wound their way through the back roads leading to the river. The crew, led by paramedic Jake Scott and EMT Molly Ferguson, had handled dozens of accidents in the area, but there was always a different urgency when the call involved someone they knew—and everyone knew Emma.

Erin stood at the water's edge, cradling Emma's head in her lap. Her jeans were soaked up to her knees, her hands trembling as she stroked Emma's damp hair. Teddy, the blind mule, stood vigil beside them, his large ears twitching at every sound. The animal had refused to leave Emma's side since Erin had dragged her from the water.

The rescue team barely had time to put the truck in park before Jake was out of the vehicle, rushing toward them with his medic bag slung over one shoulder.

"What happened?" he asked, dropping to his knees beside Erin and Emma.

"She—she fell," Erin stammered, trying to catch her breath. "She was fishing, and I-I found her like this."

Jake placed two fingers against Emma's neck, feeling for a pulse—strong, steady. Good. "Emma?" he said firmly, lightly tapping her cheek. "Emma, can you hear me?"

A weak groan was her only response.

Molly pulled out a blood pressure cuff while Jake checked her pupils with a penlight. "Pupils are equal, reactive," he reported. "No obvious skull fractures. Molly, let's check for any other injuries before we move her."

Erin hovered anxiously as the medics worked, carefully feeling for broken bones, pressing gently along Emma's ribs, legs, and arms. There was a lump forming on the back of her head, but no visible cuts or major trauma.

"She had a concussion about a month ago," Erin blurted out, her voice shaking. "And... a kidney transplant. Just a month ago."

Jake's expression sharpened. "Good to know. We'll be extra careful with her vitals and hydration levels."

"She may have a concussion," Molly said. "We'll get her stabilized and take her to Cannon Memorial."

Jake reached for the backboard. "Let's get her loaded."

As they lifted Emma onto the stretcher, Teddy let out a low, distressed bray, stomping his hooves in protest. Erin had to wrap her arms around the mule's neck to keep him from interfering.

"It's okay, Teddy," she whispered. "They're going to help her."

Emma stirred slightly as they secured her to the stretcher, her eyes fluttering open for just a moment. "Wha—"

"Shh," Erin soothed, brushing damp hair away from her daughter's face. "You're okay, sweetheart. We're taking you to the hospital."

The ambulance doors slammed shut, and within seconds, they were speeding toward Cannon Memorial Hospital.

***

The emergency room was busy for a weekday morning, but the nurses moved quickly when the ambulance doors opened. Dr. Andrew Green, a seasoned physician with a calm demeanor and sharp eye, was already waiting when they wheeled Emma in.

"What do we have?" he asked, walking beside the stretcher as they moved her into a trauma bay.

"Twenty-four-year-old female found unconscious by the river. No obvious fractures, just a contusion on the back of her head," Jake reported. "Patient had a concussion a month ago and a kidney transplant recently."

Dr. Green nodded, stepping forward as the medics transferred Emma to the hospital bed. "Emma, can you hear me?"

Her eyelids fluttered, her gaze unfocused. "Mmm."

"We're going to take care of you," he said, checking her reflexes, pressing lightly along her skull to gauge her response. "Do you know where you are?"

Emma's brow furrowed. "Hospital?"

"That's right. Do you remember what happened?"

Emma's lips parted, but then she winced, closing her eyes again. "Fishing... I fell."

Dr. Green exchanged a glance with the nurse. "We're going to run a CT scan just to be safe, but from what I'm seeing, there's no immediate concern about a skull fracture or brain bleed."

Erin, who had been standing at the foot of the bed, let out a shaky breath. "So she'll be okay?"

"I believe so, but I'd like to keep her overnight for observation to make sure she doesn't develop any worsening symptoms," Dr. Green said. "Concussions can be tricky, and we want to monitor her kidney function as well."

Erin nodded quickly. "Whatever she needs."

Emma's eyes opened again, this time more alert. She looked from Dr. Green to Erin. "Did you call work?"

Erin let out a short, incredulous laugh. "Work is the last thing you need to worry about right now."

But the question was answered soon enough when a familiar voice sounded from the doorway.

"Already handled," said Jean McPherson, stepping into the room. The director of Avery County 911 Service was a woman of presence—broad-shouldered, steady, and kind. She had taken Emma under her wing when she'd first started at the call center, helping her transition back into work after everything she'd been through.

When Jean had heard about the accident, there was no question—she had to see Emma for herself.

"Well, you sure know how to get everyone's attention," Jean teased gently as she approached the bedside. "You had us all worried."

Emma offered a weak smile. "Didn't mean to."

Jean settled into the chair beside her. "How are you feeling?"

"Like I lost a fight with a riverbank."

Jean chuckled. "That's about what I figured."

They sat in comfortable silence for a moment before Jean spoke again. "You scared your mama, you know."

Emma glanced at Erin, who was still watching her like a hawk. "Yeah," she murmured. "I know."

Jean patted her hand. "Get some rest, kid. We'll see you back at work when you're ready."

***

The night passed in slow, quiet moments. Erin refused to leave Emma's side, curling up in the chair beside her bed, stirring each time Emma shifted. Nurses came and went, checking vitals, shining penlights into her eyes, and making quiet notes on their charts.

Emma drifted in and out of sleep, the ache in her head persistent but manageable. Each time she opened her eyes, Erin was there.

"You should go home," Emma whispered at one point, her voice raspy.

Erin shook her head. "Not happening."

So Emma didn't argue.

Morning arrived with the scent of stale coffee and the soft beeping of machines. Dr. Green checked her one last time, nodding in satisfaction.

"Well, Emma, looks like you're free to go," he said. "Just take it easy for the next few days, and if you have any dizziness, nausea, or worsening headaches, you come right back in, understand?"

Emma gave a slow nod. "Understood."

By mid-morning, Erin was guiding Emma out of the hospital doors. "Let's get you home."

And Teddy would be waiting.

Chapter 20

The Decision

The morning sun spilled golden light over the Blue Ridge Mountains as Emma parked her Jeep outside the Avery County 911 Center. The air was crisp, tinged with the scent of damp earth and pine, the remnants of last night's rain still clinging to the leaves. She took a deep breath, steadying herself before stepping inside. It had been a week since her fall in the river, and though her body had healed, she still felt the weight of everything pressing on her—her job, her future, her heart.

As she settled into her shift, the familiar hum of the dispatch center wrapped around her like a well-worn jacket. The quiet murmur of voices, the occasional burst of static from the radios, and the rhythmic tapping of keyboards created a strange sense of comfort. But she knew change was coming.

"Emma," Jean McPherson's voice cut through the room. The director stood in the doorway to her office, her presence as commanding as ever. "Can I see you for a minute?"

Emma nodded, pushing back from her desk and following Jean inside. The office smelled of coffee and old books, a scent that had become familiar over the past few weeks.

Jean gestured for her to sit, then leaned against the edge of her desk, arms crossed. "You've been doing great work here," she started, her sharp gaze softening. "And I know your return to Raleigh is coming up soon."

Emma swallowed, her hands clasped in her lap. "Yeah... it is."

Jean nodded. "I wanted to talk to you before that happens. We could use you here full time. You're a natural, and I see how much this job means to you."

Emma's heart thumped against her ribs. She had known this was coming, but hearing it out loud made it real. "Jean, I-I appreciate that. More than I can say. But I..." She hesitated, running a hand through her hair. "I don't know if I'm ready to go back to Raleigh PD. Being a patrol officer again after everything..."

Jean's expression remained understanding. "Then don't force yourself to. This is your life, Emma. You get to choose what comes next."

Emma let out a slow breath. "I just—I don't know if I'm making the right decision. I love it here. I love being close to my mom, and..."

Jean's eyes twinkled knowingly. "And Dave?"

Emma felt heat rise to her cheeks but didn't deny it.

Jean smiled. "Look, whatever you decide, just make sure it's what you want, not what you think you should do."

Emma nodded slowly. "I'll think about it."

The drive home felt longer than usual, the weight of the decision pressing against her chest. The farm came into view, a picture of home she wasn't sure she was ready to leave. The scent of freshly turned soil and the distant whinny of a horse greeted her as she stepped out of the Jeep.

Inside, Erin stood by the stove, stirring a pot of soup. The rich, savory aroma of chicken and herbs filled the kitchen. She glanced up, immediately reading the conflict on her daughter's face. "What's wrong?"

Emma dropped into a chair, rubbing her temples. "Jean offered me a full-time job."

Erin stilled for a moment, then set the spoon down. "And?"

Emma exhaled. "And I don't know what to do. I'm supposed to go back to Raleigh, back to being an officer. But I don't think I can. Not yet. Maybe not ever."

Erin wiped her hands on a towel and sat across from her. "Sweetheart, you don't have to go back. No one's making you."

"I know," Emma murmured. "But what if I'm letting people down?"

Erin reached across the table, taking Emma's hands in hers. "The only person you need to worry about letting down is yourself."

Emma swallowed hard. "And then there's Dave."

Erin smiled knowingly. "I've seen the way he looks at you, Emma. That man cares about you. If he's worth it, he'll support whatever choice you make."

Emma let the words sink in. Deep down, she knew her mother was right.

Needing air, she grabbed her jacket and stepped outside. The farm stretched before her, its rolling hills bathed in the afternoon light. Teddy, the aging blind mule, perked his ears at her approach, falling into step beside her as she walked toward the river.

"Alright, old man," she murmured, scratching behind his ears. "What would you do?"

Teddy snorted, nudging her side as if to say, *Stay.*

She walked in silence, taking in the rustling leaves, the distant chirp of crickets, and the cool breeze carrying the scent of damp earth and wildflowers. When she reached the riverbank, she sat down, letting her fingers trace the smooth stones beside her.

The water flowed, steady and unbothered, shifting and changing as it always had. Her father's words echoed in her mind: *Life is a lot like this river. It is never the same water; it always changes. You have to be willing to accept those changes, and who knows, you may even find a keeper the next time you put your line in.*

Emma closed her eyes. Change wasn't easy. But maybe it wasn't supposed to be.

By the time she got back to the house, she knew what she had to do. She picked up the phone, her fingers hovering over the screen before she dialed Chief Williams' number.

The call went straight through. "Patterson," the chief greeted, his voice gruff but warm. "How are you feeling?"

Emma took a steadying breath. "I'm better, sir. But I need to talk to you about my return."

There was a pause. "Go on."

"I don't think I can come back," she admitted. "I've been working with Dr. Lawson, trying to manage the PTSD from the shooting at Mac's. But I'm not ready to be back on patrol. And my mom needs me here."

The chief was quiet for a long moment before he finally spoke. "I understand, Emma. You've been through a lot. You need to do what's right for you."

Relief washed over her. "Thank you, Chief."

"You ever change your mind, you know where to find me," he said gruffly.

She smiled. "Yes, sir."

As she hung up, a weight lifted. It was done.

But now, she had to tell Dave.

Her chest tightened at the thought. Would he understand? Would he stay?

These were her worries, but as she looked out over the farm, the river, the home she loved—she knew one thing for certain.

She was right where she belonged.

***

Meanwhile, in Raleigh, Dave sat in a squad car with Detective Raines, watching the city bustle past them. It felt strange to be back on normal duty after his time with the drug task force. Stranger still was the uncertainty that gnawed at him.

Would Emma come back?

What if she didn't?

Raines glanced at him. "You've been quiet."

Dave exhaled, rubbing a hand over his jaw. "Just got a lot on my mind."

"Emma?" Raines guessed.

Dave nodded. "Yeah. She's supposed to come back, but… what if she doesn't?"

Raines was quiet for a moment before he spoke. "And what if she does? Could you watch her go back out there and risk her life again? Could you handle seeing her in danger, knowing what happened last time?"

Dave clenched his jaw. "I don't know."

Raines nodded as if he understood more than he let on. "Love makes things complicated."

Dave stared out the window, watching the city roll past.

Complicated didn't even begin to cover it.

Chapter 21

It's a Date

The evening air was crisp, carrying the scent of damp earth and pine as Dave drove up the winding gravel road toward the farmhouse. The sound of his truck's tires crunching over loose stones echoed in the stillness. Inside, Emma stood in front of the mirror, smoothing down the soft fabric of her floral dress. It felt strange to wear something so delicate after months of living in work uniforms and denim, but tonight was special.

Erin popped her head in, her eyes twinkling with warmth. "He's here," she said with a knowing smile. "And you look... happy."

Emma turned, adjusting a stray curl behind her ear. "I am happy, Mom."

Erin tilted her head. "Love suits you."

Downstairs, Dave stepped onto the porch and knocked on the door. Erin opened it, greeting him with her usual warmth. "Come on in, Dave."

As Dave stepped inside, the familiar scent of home—woodsmoke, vanilla, and something faintly herbal—wrapped around him. And then Emma appeared at the top of the staircase. His breath hitched. She looked radiant, the soft fabric of her dress flowing as she descended, her eyes sparkling in the dim light.

"Wow," he murmured, rubbing the back of his neck. "You look…" He trailed off, searching for words that did her justice.

Emma smirked. "I'll take 'Wow.'"

Dave chuckled, stepping forward to take her hand. "Ready?"

She nodded, her fingers curling around his. As they stepped outside, the cool night air was alive with the sounds of cicadas and the distant call of an owl. The drive to The Stag & Thistle was quiet and comfortable, the road winding through the darkened mountains.

When they arrived, the pub was buzzing with life. The scent of aged wood, ale, and hearty food filled the air, mingling with the soft strains of a fiddle playing in the background. A warm glow from the lanterns cast golden hues over the crowd.

They settled into a small, cozy table near the fireplace. "What'll you have?" Dave asked, scanning the drink menu.

Emma grinned. "A Johnnie & Ginger."

Dave raised an eyebrow. "Fancy."

"Classic," she corrected with a wink.

Dave smirked and turned to the bartender. "Glenlivet neat for me."

The drinks arrived, the rich, smoky scent of whiskey rising from Dave's glass, mingling with the sharp ginger and warm Scotch in Emma's. She took a sip, the burn spreading through her chest, sweetened by the wine.

Daniel, the pub's owner, walked by, and Dave grinned. "Emma tells me you recite 'Tam O'Shanter'?"

Daniel's face lit up. "Aye, that I do. You in the mood for some Burns?"

The pub quieted as Daniel took center stage, his voice weaving through the dramatic tale, each word dripping with emotion. The room hung on every syllable; the clink of glasses momentarily stilled. As he finished, the crowd erupted into applause, and Dave signaled to the bartender. "A pint for the poet."

Dinner followed. The rich, savory aroma of shepherd's pie filling the space as they dug into their meal. The crust was golden and flaky, the filling steaming with tender lamb and vegetables. They ended with a decadent slice of chocolate cake, its bittersweet richness melting on their tongues.

The band struck up a lively tune, and Dave held out a hand. "Dance with me?"

Emma hesitated. "I'm not the best dancer."

"Good," Dave said with a grin. "Neither am I."

They moved together on the worn wooden floor, laughter mixing with the music. The warmth of Dave's hand against hers, the firm pressure of his arm around her waist—it was grounding, safe. The music slowed, and for a moment, the world shrank to just the two of them.

As closing time neared, the entire pub joined in a rendition of "Auld Lang Syne." The lyrics, sung with both cheer and melancholy, struck a chord deep in Emma's chest. She blinked away tears, but Dave's voice rose, strong and unrestrained, lifting the mood as he sang with infectious energy. She laughed, nudging him playfully.

Outside, the night was cool, the scent of fresh pine and distant rain in the air. The drive home was quiet, filled with the gentle hum of the radio and the occasional stolen glance.

Back at the farmhouse, Erin was still awake, the glow of the television flickering in the living room. She greeted them with a knowing look. "Dave, you're welcome to stay in the guest room. No sense in driving back this late."

Dave hesitated. "I wouldn't want to impose—"

"Nonsense," Erin said, standing. "Goodnight, you two."

Emma turned to Dave, nerves fluttering in her stomach. He reached out, brushing his knuckles lightly against her cheek. "I had a great time tonight."

"Me too," she whispered.

He leaned in, and the kiss that followed was slow, unhurried, lingering in the quiet space between them. When they pulled apart, Emma's cheeks were flushed, her breath uneven.

Dave smiled, his voice low. "Goodnight, Emma."

"Goodnight, Dave."

And with that, they went their separate ways—each carrying the warmth of the night with them.

Chapter 22

New Beginnings

The scent of fresh hay, warm animal musk, and faint traces of molasses filled the air as Emma pushed open the heavy wooden barn doors. Sunlight streamed in through the slats in the old structure, casting golden streaks across the packed dirt floor. Dust motes danced in the beams of light, creating a soft, hazy glow over the familiar surroundings.

Emma inhaled deeply, savoring the carthy scent that spoke of home. She turned to Teddy, who stood at her side, his gray muzzle twitching as he caught the smells of the barn. "Come on, old boy," she murmured, scratching between his ears before stepping further inside.

The gentle rustling of animals stirring greeted her ears as she made her way to the milking area. Lucy, precocious as always, nipped at her jeans at the sight of her, her big brown eyes filled with expectation. Next to her, Ethel, her true companion, shifted on her hooves, eager for her turn to be milked.

Behind her, the steady crunch of boots on straw signaled Dave's arrival. "This place has a certain charm," he said, his voice laced with admiration as he took in the rustic space. "Never thought I'd find myself in a barn at sunrise, but I could get used to this."

Emma grinned, reaching for the metal pail and the clean cloths hanging on the nearby wooden peg. "It's peaceful, isn't it?" she said, wiping Lucy's udder with practiced care. "I grew up to the rhythm of this barn—morning milking, afternoon feedings, evening chores. It's funny how it all just feels… right."

Dave watched as Lucy stepped onto the milking platform with practiced ease, settling into her usual spot. Emma knelt beside her, her fingers working with smooth efficiency as she coaxed milk into the stainless-steel bucket. The steady hiss and squirt of milk hitting the pail echoed through the barn, a comforting, rhythmic sound.

Dave picked up a scoop of grain from a nearby barrel and placed it in Lucy's feed bucket. "Figured she'd appreciate a little breakfast," he said with a wink.

Emma chuckled, "Smart man. Happy goats give more milk."

Dave leaned against a nearby beam, watching her hands move with quiet skill. "You make it look easy," he observed.

"It's all about the rhythm," Emma replied. "Gentle but firm, never rushed." She glanced up at him with a teasing smile. "Want to try?"

He hesitated, then crouched beside her. "Alright, show me how."

Emma took his hands, guiding them over Lucy's udder. "Thumb and forefinger first, then squeeze with the rest of your hand, like this."

Dave followed her lead, and a thin stream of milk spurted into the pail. "Well, would you look at that? I'm a natural," he joked.

Emma laughed. "You might have a future in dairy farming yet."

Lucy let out a contented sigh, chewing her grain as Dave continued under Emma's watchful eye. After a few more attempts, Emma took over, quickly finishing the milking. When the pail was nearly full, she handed it to Dave. "Here, go ahead and strain it into the jar."

Dave carried the bucket over to the counter, carefully pouring the milk through the fine-mesh strainer and into a large Mason jar. The creamy liquid flowed smoothly, catching the golden morning light as it filled the container. He twisted on the plastic lid and placed it in the small fridge against the barn wall.

By the time he turned back, Emma had already helped Lucy down and guided Ethel onto the platform. She wiped down the Alpine's udder, then settled in for another round.

Dave grabbed a clean bucket and crouched next to her, cleaning the first pail with a nearby rag. As he worked, he found himself watching her, admiring the quiet grace with which she moved. Her hands, calloused but gentle, her expression one of quiet focus.

He reached out and rubbed a soothing circle over the small of her back, pressing a kiss against the nape of her neck. "You amaze me, you know that?"

Emma stilled for just a second before turning to kiss him softly. "You're not so bad yourself, city boy," she murmured before finishing Ethel's milking.

Dave took the fresh bucket from her hands and repeated the straining and storing process. As he sealed the second jar, he turned to find Emma watching him, her expression thoughtful.

"You're really staying, huh?" he asked, his voice softer now.

She nodded, glancing around the barn before meeting his gaze. "Yeah. This is home. And I want to be here."

A slow smile spread across Dave's face. "I think I like the sound of that."

Emma wiped her hands on a rag and stretched. "Well, chores are done." She started toward the door, but Dave cocked an eyebrow.

"Wait a minute, aren't there more?" he teased. "I was promised an authentic farm experience."

Emma smirked. "Not today." She disappeared inside the house, leaving the screen door swinging behind her.

Curious, Dave followed, only to find her waiting just inside the doorway, holding two fishing rods and a vest. She handed them to him with a grin. "Here, this is for you."

Dave took the rod and vest, slipping it on as they headed toward the river, Teddy ambling along behind them.

Not the end of their story—just the beginning.

As you reach the final page of this journey, I want to extend my heartfelt gratitude for accompanying me through this story. Your support means the world to me. As a token of appreciation, I invite you to visit www.outerridgepress.com. There you can claim a special gift crafted just for readers like you. This exclusive offering is my way of saying thank you and sharing a piece of the story's essence beyond the pages. I hope it brings you as much joy as writing this novel has brought me.

About the Author

Rebecca G. Hooper

Rebecca G. Hooper is a storyteller at heart, drawn to the quiet magic of small towns and the deeply human moments that bind us together. Originally from Houston, Texas, she now calls North Carolina home—a place that has captured her heart and become the inspiration behind her debut novella, *Keepers*.

Set in the picturesque Blue Ridge Mountains, *Keepers* is the first in a heartfelt series that explores the power of love, community, and emotional connection. Through richly layered characters and feel-good storytelling, Hooper invites readers into a world where relationships matter, and every story is a gentle reminder of what it means to belong.

When she's not writing, Rebecca enjoys discovering local gems tucked into mountain towns, reading swoon-worthy romances, and soaking in the simple joys of Southern life. Her characters may live on the page, but they're born from the same spirit that lives in all of us—a longing to love and be loved, to connect, and to come home.